THE GOBLIN'S EYES

THE GOBLIN CHRONICLES BOOK 1

SORCHA MONK

No frogs nor toads were harmed in the writing of this book.

First edition 2024

Main image cover artist: Jordna

Background and formatting cover artist: getcovers.com

ebook ISBN: 978-1-961616-03-5

hardcover ISBN: 978-1-961616-05-9

paperback ISBN: 978-1-961616-04-2

If you have a friend who is a goblin, you probably know that goblins have rules about writing and reading and giving them your name... (you *haven't* given them your name, have you?). Anyway, if you really are a good friend to a goblin, which would be odd but still very possible, you should read this to them. Because they can't. Because: rules.

Spot Ox Publishing

Sorcha Monk

If you have your mother's eyes, or your father's ears, or grandparent's nose...

...they might appreciate it if you gave them back.

Contents

About ten years ago....

One

The goblin had her mother's eyes. She also had her grandmother's and her great-grandmother's. She kept them in a bag tied to her belt. When the time came, her own eyes would go into the bag and it would be given to her daughter. It was the tradition.

She hadn't used them this night, however. Didn't need to. It was obvious that the frog was nothing but a frog. She did regret, just a little bit, having eaten the thing. It had been plump and full of warts, and she couldn't help herself. But now her appetite was ruined for dinner.

"Eh," she muttered, quaffing the last of the ale in the jug. The girl had brought three of them. Jugs, that is, not frogs. The goblin let out a long belch. "And that's why you always take payment in advance, isn't it?" she goblin said to nobody because, except for the pig, there was nobody else around. She tossed the empty jug in the ditch.

The goblin uncorked the second jug, poured some into a bowl for the pig, and scratched the pink swine between the ears as it slurped the bowl empty. The cork shoved back in place, she put the second and third jugs in the bag slung across the pig's back, hitched up her burlap trousers (rough and itchy, dirty and with a stench woven into the threads – just as a goblin's trousers should be), and climbed aboard.

Looking over her shoulder one last time, she watched the crying girl disappear around the bend. The goblin stuck a long and crooked fingernail in her mouth and plucked a piece of frog bone from between her teeth. She shook her head, her ears flapping against her cheeks. "Stupid girl… frogs ain't princes and princes ain't frogs." But even so, she felt a twinge of pity. A very slight twinge, but more than most goblins usually had to endure.

The goblin sighed as she stuck her thumb-claw in her ear and pulled out a chunk of wax that smelled as bad as it looked. She pulled one of the few hairs from her pale, spotted head and rolled it with the wax until it was a pebble in between her fingers. A hollow reed was retrieved from somewhere in the folds of her body.

She paused. Then she grumbled. She slipped the hair-wax-pebble into the hollowed center and, putting the reed to her disheveled lips, she muttered, "git home safe." And she blew.

The hair-wax-pebble flew through the air, accompanied by copious spittle. Down the road, the girl stopped, wiped the back of her neck and inspected the stinking glop that had hit her. She already felt cruelly disappointed, and now she was downright disgusted. But she would get home safely that night.

A tap of the goblin's toes let the pig know it was time to go home, and it turned and trotted along a path only it and its rider could see.

After a ride that was neither annoyingly short nor horrendously long, they reached the foot of a hill made entirely of rock. The pig was sent to happily rummage for food, and the goblin went inside the cave that she called home. It was cold and musty. The floor was covered with sharp twigs and pieces of gnawed bones and rotted flesh. The walls were grimy, and the lone chair was covered with more ash and dust than the fireplace in front of it. A pot of something that smelled like it had died at least twice was boiling over the fire, and a small black and white bird was stirring it with a wooden ladle.

"Hmmph…" the goblin muttered.

"What?" The bird stopped stirring. "You didn't eat the frog, did you? You'll've ruined your appetite."

The goblin sat in her chair, dust puffing up then settling back in place. Whatever was in the pot had a deliciously malodorous aroma, and she decided that, frog in her belly or no frog in her belly, she was going to have some dinner.

"I've got room," she said.

The magpie ladled swill into a wooden bowl and gave it to the goblin. "The moth came by today," it said.

"Mphhmph…" The old goblin slurped her porridge and didn't look up

"It was a request."

"Mphhmph…"

"There's a pregnant woman who wants to meet with you. Needs to know whether her child is going to be a boy."

"Spfft!" The goblin spluttered and nearly gakked on the wad of whatever it was that was sliding down her throat. "What's that you say?"

"A pregnant woman wants to know if it's a boy," the bird snickered.

"Uh-huh…" the goblin scratched her pocked chin.

It was dangerous for a pregnant woman to meet with a goblin. Goblins had an excellent sense of smell, and it didn't matter that the baby was still inside the mother's belly. The aroma of sweet, soft tissue, unfinished organs, and the fluids that surrounded it were irresistible. More than one expectant mother had returned home from meeting a goblin without her baby, inside or out. And it'd been a long time since this goblin had tasted a delicious infant.

"And what was the offering?"

"Anything you want." The bird flapped its wings and hopped onto the small stack of firewood.

"You don't say…"

Equally dangerous was an offer of *anything you want* because a goblin had many things they wanted. Humans made the mistake of believing it would be gold or silver. But there were other things a goblin desired. Unimaginable things.

This made the goblin suspicious.

"Why such an offer?" she raised an eyebrow of three scraggly hairs.

"The woman is the wife of a king across the river, and she needs to know because, if it's not a boy, she'll have to run away. The king's beheaded his last two wives who didn't give him a son."

"Why doesn't she just leave now? He don't sound like a good husband at all."

"Maybe living like a queen is worth it," the bird shrugged and preened the feathers of one wing.

The goblin watched the embers in the fire and thought for a while. Something didn't feel right about all of this.

"I'll ruminate on it," she said and rose from the chair, her bones creaking almost as much as the relieved piece of furniture.

She spat into the fire and scratched herself in a few places the magpie had rather not seen, flatulating an impressive amount of intestinal air as her nails dug into the thick skin. She ambled across the room and laid down on the pile of straw she called her bed, the bag of eyeballs held firmly between her leathery hands, and closed her eyes.

Cocking its head from side to side, the magpie watched the old goblin for a few minutes, waiting until she was just getting into the deep river of sleep.

"Wock!" The magpie shouted.

The goblin nearly jumped out of her thick, warted skin. "Blasted bird!" she yelled, reaching around for something to throw at it.

"Wock!" the magpie said again. "Don't you want to hear the rest of it?"

"Sppaffatt!" Unable to find anything to throw, the goblin spat at the bird. "The rest of what?" Angrily, she rolled over to face away from the nuisance.

"The moth's message, of course."

The goblin rolled back and up. "There's more?"

"Yes."

"Why didn't you say so before?"

"You were enjoying your dinner so much – "

"Tell me!" the goblin growled. "Tell me now, you despicable excuse for a corvid. Or you'll be magpie stew before tomorrow."

"The queen will be under the likho tree when the moon is full."

"What?"

"The quee—"

"I heard you!" the goblin snapped. She got up and began walking circles, the cave being too small to pace back and forth, muttering an argument with herself. Her flat feet slapped the ground and the nails of her long toes tapped the hard dirt with each step.

The magpie hopped to the wooden bowl, surveying the leftover morsels.

"Full moon's tomorrow night," the goblin groused, "and the likho tree's on the other side of the river."

The magpie tossed something green in the air, caught it with its pointed black beak and swallowed it down.

"Even if I could make it, no goblins *ever* go to the likho tree." She clenched her long-fingered fists. "No smart ones, at least."

"Weer-weer-weer," the magpie chittered. "Anything you want…"

The goblin stopped. She mumbled a bit more, then spat on the floor and announced, "We're going."

"We?"

The bag of eyeballs retied to her belt, the goblin started searching around the cave.

"Magpies don't go out in the dark," the bird protested.

"You can be my eyes and ears." The goblin kicked at a pile of bones and looked under the rug made of the stitched hides of various vermin.

"You have a bag of eyes and your ears are bigger than any I've ever seen. You don't need me."

"You can watch the pig." Wooden pots and mugs flew across the room as the search continued.

"The pig doesn't need watching as long as there's something around for it to eat."

"Ah!" Finding what she was looking for, the goblin grabbed her red cap from under the pile of shiny magpie treasure. She turned to the bird. "You're going with me because I'm sayin' you are and that's that."

The goblin marched out of the cave.

The bird hesitated for a moment, then flew to catch up.

Two

*T*he gnarled tree crouched at the top of a low hill. A ferocious head of leafless twigs shot up from its neck, and two thickly knotted branches stuck out from either side of its torso. Just above the surface of the grassy knoll it bifurcated into a pair of substantial roots that anchored it to the ground. In the full moon's light, the tendrils of its malevolent shadow strained in every direction like ill-behaved offspring. Only a little bit of moonlight was able to squeeze through, but it was enough to show a very pregnant woman standing beneath the tree.

A short distance away, the goblin hid behind a large rock. The pig had been left behind in a shallow mudpuddle at the river's edge. It was better not to have her ride home too close to the likho tree. "Ahhh…" she said, inhaling the scent of the unborn baby wafting towards them. "The only thing better than the smell of a human infant is the taste of one."

11

The magpie perched on the boulder, transfixed by something shiny wrapped around the woman's ankle. The goblin saw where it was looking.

"Don't you dare!"

"But I must have it."

"No! You'll scare her off. You can have it after."

"Fine." The bird hunched down and squatted on the rock. "But you'd better not be lying."

"You'd better watch the words that come out of your beak..." the goblin growled, knowing very well that she probably *was* lying. She hadn't decided yet.

Sulking, but still enamored by the shiny little chain, the bird hopped down and rode on the goblin's globuled rump as she belly-crawled, silently slithering towards the tree. When close enough, she jumped and grabbed the startled woman around the neck. The magpie jumped off the goblin's rear to snatch the anklet.

They pulled, but the chain around the woman's leg was held firmly in the hands of the goblin hiding on the other side of the tree.

The two goblins stared at each other, one sneering while the other smiled a row of jagged teeth, while the magpie pulled harder on the chain. The woman looked at the three of them, preparing to say something, but before she could speak a word the four of them were swooped up and suspended in the air, held by misshapen hands of rough bark. The likho, also known as a goblin-tree, strode across the glen with its treasure.

"Ouch!" the goblin snarled and dug her teeth into the twig twisting around her belly. "Watch where you're putting your thorns, you rotted piece of wood. You'll be tinder for my fire before this's all over." She turned to the red-capped hobgoblin wrapped in a netting of twig-fingers. "You had to meet under the likho tree, didn't you!"

"Of course I did, Edwina," her estranged husband answered.

The magpie cocked its head. It wasn't often that someone used the goblin's name. Partly because names weren't mean to be shared willy-nilly, and partly because there were very few people, goblins or otherwise, who wanted to talk to the cranky old hag.

"That was a long time ago," Edwina snapped back. She curled into the branches carrying her and sulked for a bit, then said, "Where'd you get the pregnant woman?"

"Found her wandering in a field downriver," answered Morris. (Morris was her husband's name.)

"I wasn't wandering!" they heard the woman say from somewhere down below. "I was tending the sheep." They ignored her.

"You always knew how to lure me out," Edwina smiled, in spite of herself. "Of course I knew it wasn't no queen nohow."

"A queen?" the woman shouted, "If I was a queen do you think I'd still be here with you?"

"Yes," Morris said.

"Woot," the magpie called from one of the topmost tree-fists. "Can I have that chain when you're done with it?"

The tree trundled across the valley, towards the woods.

"I know what you're after, Morris," Edwina muttered, just loud enough for her husband to hear.

"Then why don't you hand it over?"

"It ain'tn't time yet."

"Her birthday's next week. Tradition's tradition."

14

"I'm still using my own eyes, thank you very much. Hey! Watch the thorns!" Edwina slapped at the offending branch again.

"Yoo-hoo!" the woman called, "what do I have to do with all of this?"

"Nothing to do with you," the magpie answered. "Just your baby."

"What's my baby got to do with it?"

The magpie cocked its head sideways. "Woot. Do you really want to know?"

"Hush! All of you!" The goblin-tree shook every branch on its body. "You're giving me a headache."

"You could let us go," the bird suggested.

"Nah," the tree said. "Family's coming over for stew tonight, and you're the perfect ingredients."

"Come on, Edwina. It's her turn." Morris crooned.

"Nope. Not yet."

"Confound it, you old hag of a goblin woman!"

"Flattery will get you nowhere."

"Does anyone feel like telling me what's going on?" the woman called up.

Morris crossed his arms, scowled, and looked away from his wife.

Edwina crossed her arms, glowered at her husband, and looked in the other direction.

"It's all about that sack of eyeballs on the goblin's belt," the magpie said.

'Which goblin?"

"Me," said Edwina. "And it's gonna stay on my belt until I say it don't."

"It's supposed to go to her daughter on her birthday," the bird continued, "and she doesn't want to give it up. I guess that part's obvious."

"Yes, I can see she's attached to it. Why?" Then the woman said, "Wait. Did you say eyeballs?"

"They're my mum's," said Edwina, "and her mum's and her mum's and hers and so on back as far as the family's hags go."

"And now it's Mildred's turn to get the bag," Morris said, still looking away.

"Who's Mildred?"

"Her daughter," said the magpie.

"So," the woman tried to work it out. "You," she tried to point but her hands were held tight by the rough twig-hand. "Morris caught me to lure Edwina out and to try and get the bag from her. But Edwina doesn't want to give it up yet."

"That's pretty much it," said the magpie. "And I'm getting that chain when it's all over and done."

"Hmph!" Morris scoffed.

"Wait a minute," said the woman. "Are you goblins or hobgoblins?"

"Both," said Morris.

"Hobgoblins is a branch of goblins," said Edwina.

"The wording's more or less interchangeable in our neck of the woods," explained Morris.

The woman thought for a moment, then asked, "And how am I a lure?"

"I told you, it's not you. It's the baby inside."

The woman looked down at her belly, then up towards the goblin woman. "You wouldn't!"

"Oh-hoh! Wouldn't I! It's been years since I've had a baby." Edwina considered her words and laughed, "Years since eatin' one. Even more years since birthin' one."

"Those are just horror stories."

"No," said Morris. "It's all true."

The woman grew silent, trying to remember all the tales her mother and grandmother had told her.

Edwina and Morris grew silent, mulling how angry they were at the other.

The magpie watched as the likho's long strides brought them closer and closer to the woods.

Three

"*W*hat's that smell?" the woman wrinkled her nose in disgust.

Morris looked out through the wooden bars of the cage where they had been unceremoniously tossed. "Broth for the stew," he said.

"It doesn't smell like any broth I've ever made," she pulled up a fold of her skirt and tried to bury her nose in it.

"You've never made stew like a goblin does," said Edwina.

The magpie hopped onto the woman's foot and began pulling at the chain around her ankle. She kicked him off.

"Goblins like treasures, don't they?" the woman asked. "Isn't there anything we can trade with him? It? You know… in exchange for letting us go?"

"The likho goblin ain't like other goblins," said Edwina.

"But, surely, there's something," the woman said, eyeing the bag on Edwina's belt.

"Oh, no you don't! Don't even think about it."

"What good's it gonna do you if you're in a pot of stew?"

"She's right," said Morris.

"You'd say anything to get this bag for Mildred," Edwina scoffed.

"Tell me again," the woman tried to sound calm, "why don't you want to give it to your daughter. Mildred, is it?"

"Yes, Mildred," said Morris. "It's because she's selfish, that's why!"

"Blast the day I met you, you old buttered hobgoblin!" Edwina screeched. "I'd've never had a daughter and this bag'd be mine forever's."

"You don't mean that."

Edwina glared at her husband an extra amount of time, for good measure, then said to the woman, "When a goblin girl gets to a certain age she gets the bag. And she gets her mother's eyes."

"You mean – "

"My eyes go in the bag when she gets it. But I'm still usin' them!"

"Well, I can see the problem…" the woman said.

"Woot. Good one."

"I didn't mean it that way."

"Still good," chittered the bird.

"Does it have to be *your* eyes?" the woman asked.

"It's always been that way," said Edwina. "It's tradition."

"Bah, tradition," the woman said. "I've broken more traditions than my father will ever know."

Morris sat up. "Tradition is tradition!"

Edwina ignored him. "I hadn't thought of it that way."

"Yes," the woman said, "maybe it could be any eyes."

"Could be the father's," Edwina looked at her husband.

"Needs to be the female's eyes," he said, scooting away from his wife.

"Says who?"

"You know," said the magpie, "there's another set of eyes you could use."

"Not mine," the woman shielded her face, then her belly. "Not the baby's either."

Edwina inhaled. A bit of drool dripped from her lip.

"You're not eating my baby!" The woman stood and put up her fists.

"Heh!" Morris laughed. "Will ya look at her?"

"Reminds me of myself," Edwina chuckled.

"I wasn't going to say it," Morris said, "not out loud, at least."

"Hullo?" the bird interrupted. "Does anyone want to know what I'm talking about?"

"Not usually," said Edwina.

"I'll listen," said the woman.

"The likho. It's got eyes, doesn't it?"

The woman and the two goblins turned to look at the huge goblin standing over the boiling pot, stirring the contents with its gnarled hand.

"And how do you suggest we get them?"

"Do I get the chain?"

"Yes," said Morris, "you can have the chain, *if* you get us out of here."

"Wouldn't do me much good if we weren't out of here, would it?"

"You wretched bird," Edwina barked, "just tell us."

"You see that plank of wood on the wall there?" the magpie said to the woman. "Can you reach it?"

"Yes, but I don't see how –"

"And do you have any chalk with you? In your pocket or somewhere?" As a master thief, the bird knew humans always carried things in their pockets. Chalk was often one of those things.

The woman found a pocket within the folds of her skirt and dug out a small piece of chalk. She held it up for all to see.

Edwina and Morris grew nervous. They knew what chalk was for. If a goblin's eyes fell upon writing of any sort, they would have their thoughts stolen from their heads, enslaving them and cursing their eyes forever. If they saw even a single written letter, the only way to save themselves was to wrench their cursed eyes from their sockets.

"Now, for the next part," said the magpie, "you two are gonna want to cover your eyes."

The two goblins didn't need to be told. Their eyes were already hidden between hands, feet, ear flaps and as much belly as they could dig their chins into.

"Wait a minute," said the woman. "I think I know what you're thinking, and I think I should get something out of this. Considering how I'm the only one who can do it."

"What is it?" Morris asked from behind the large hands covering his face and eyes.

"I get to keep my baby."

The likho screeched, blindly hurling tables and chairs across the cave. A brownish goo oozed from the sockets where its eyes had been. There'd been no choice. The wretched human's handwriting on the wall cursed his vision and so the eyeballs *had* to be removed. If they'd stayed put, who knows what contracts to the mists of time the woman, who most certainly must be a demon, would bind them to. The eyes had to be torn out and thrown to the ground before they infected the rest of the goblin-tree's body.

Their cage smashed, the captives climbed through the rummage and into freedom. As she escaped, Edwina found the likho's eyeballs rolling across the floor, and she scooped them up with a leathery hand and dropped them into the bag that was to be given to Mildred next week for her birthday.

"Tradition! Hah! Tradition can scag itself," Edwina laughed.

The two hobgoblins and the woman ran as fast as their feet could carry them, the magpie close behind with the silvery chain hanging from its beak. But they couldn't outrun the condemnations reverberating across the hills. Most of the expletives were foreign, even to the hobgoblins' ears. However, there was one string of words they clearly heard: "…a curse upon that thing you carry!"

Edwina looked at the woman, thinking *That's what you and your egregious offspring deserve!*

The woman looked at Edwina, thinking *That disgusting sack of eyes. A curse is what the wretched goblin deserves.*

Morris kept his eyes straight ahead, thinking *Could be either of the two, and, in the vein of self-preservation, I believe I'll be veering off from this pair of females at my first opportunity.*

The magpie admired the shiny chain clasped within its beak, gleaming in the bright sunlight, and thought only of how nice it would look atop the pile of collected trinkets back home in the goblin's cave.

A couple of months later....

Four

*T*he irritated woman opened the door with a force that ruffled the hairs of the corpulent pomp's mustache. She checked to see that his officious, ring-fingered fist hadn't knocked loose the talisman made of dog and horse hair wrapped around a piece of chalk. The last thing she wanted was to have to go back to the old witch who'd made it and get another one. The goblin repellent was expensive, and the old crone had bad breath and talked a lot. Plus there was the additional charge for anti-curse insurance. (Although the woman wasn't convinced the curse was on the heads of her newborn sons, she'd decided it was best to have the safeguard, just in case.)

"Where's the man of the house?" the taxman huffed, straightening his squirrely mustache with a finger and thumb.

"Which one?"

For a brief moment, the man was puzzled. His fingers slid down from the mustache to the equally squirrely beard, grasping it like a ratted rope. He looked up with what he believed was a twinkle of cleverness, but in reality looked like he'd developed a spasm in one eye.

"The one in charge, of course," he said, puffing out his chest and moving his hand to find the belt under his belly, hooking his thumb between it and the strained uniform.

"Well, which is it?" said the woman. "Do you want to talk to the man of the house or the one who's in charge?"

The squirrely mustache hopped up and down.

"Confound it, woman. Let me in!" The man shoved his way past her and stomped his large and dirty boots across the just-swept floor. He spied an old man sitting in a rocking chair in front of the fire.

"Ho, there. You're the man of the house?"

"Eh?" the old man put the boiled egg he was trying to crack back on the plate that was resting on his lap.

"He wants to know if you're the man of the house," said the woman. She thought of fetching the broom and sweeping up the mess in an exaggerated manner, just to make a point, but she decided against it. The taxman not only wouldn't care. He wouldn't notice. And she'd end up doing twice the sweeping after he'd left.

"Am I?" The old man's eyebrows raised with excitement at the opportunity.

"Of course you are," said the taxman.

"Awlright den," said the old man. "Hows can I help you?"

"I need the names of them two newborns." He waved an arm towards the crib at the other end of the hearth.

"Why don't you ask me?" said the woman. "I *am* their mother, you know."

"Leave us be," the taxman scolded. "Get back to your woman's work."

"Yeah," the old man chimed in, "and crack dis here egg for me."

"That's a potato, you old sot."

The old man looked at the spud. "So it is," he said, and held it to the few molars he had left and began to gnaw on it.

"Boy or girl?" With a flourish, the taxman held up the clipboard that was tied with a rope to a hidden belt loop. His fat fingers grabbed, fumbled and grabbed again the stick of black chalk that was tied to the top of the clipboard, ruining the flourishment of the moment. When he had everything ready to write, he looked up at the old man.

"What's dat?" said the old man.

"Are they boy or girl?"

"Who?"

The taxman's eager hand lost its enthusiasm and began to tremble in a different sort of emotion.

"They're twin boys," said the woman.

The taxman pretended to ignore her, but wrote it down. "And their names?" He continued to look at the old man.

"*Whose* name?" Pieces of gnawed potato flew from the old man's mouth.

"I can tell you," said the woman. "They're Cor'Nan'Deagun'Lug'Maod-Has and Ran'Ousa'Erult'Antach-Lain."

The taxman, wiping potato from his face, turned to look at the woman.

"They're named after their uncles," she said.

The squirrely monobrow twitched.

"They've lots of uncles."

Turning back to the old man, the taxman tried again to speak with the only sensible person in the room – that is, the one that was not the woman.

"If you don't mind, *sir*," with an emphasis on the *sir*, "can you tell me their names?"

"Well, lemme see." The old man pushed himself out of the rocking chair with boney arms that seemed to have too many elbows, and he shuffled over to the crib.

Two round faces looked up at their grandfather and the giant squirrel standing next to him. Newborn-blue eyes twinkled and their mouths curled into grins that would have been frightening had there been teeth behind them. In the folds of the blankets, their small fingers wriggled in gleeful imaginings of grabbing tufts of squirrel hair.

"Well," the old man pointed to one of the infants, "dere's dis-un." Then he pointed to the other one. "And dere's d'udder-un."

The taxman scribbled the names on the clipboard. He looked at the words he'd written. They didn't look like real names, but he certainly wasn't going to ask the *woman* about it. Besides, anyhow you looked at it, Dissun and Dudderun were better than Cor'Nan'Deagun'Lug'Maod-Has and Ran'Ousa'Erult'Antach-Lain. As he saw it, he was doing the boys a favor.

Sorcha Monk

And now....

Five

*I*t was the tenth annual shearing of the sheep since the twins had been born, and now they were old enough to help. So, of course, they were up in a tree overlooking the pond, far enough away to claim they were out of earshot and couldn't possibly have known they were missing out on the activities.

"What's she doin'?" Dudderun lay with his belly across a thick limb, squinting at the view across the water.

"Looks like she's kissin' frogs," said Dissun. He was in the same position as his brother, but up one branch higher.

"Poor frog," said Dudderun.

"I wonder what else she might kiss."

"I seen a skunk down in the gully."

"Nah," said Dissun, "she probly'd not kiss somethin' dead."

Dissun wasn't convinced of that, but decided talking about girls was getting boring. He looked up and asked, "D'ya think it's been long enough?"

"Sun's not barely past mid-day. They'll be doin' it 'till they can't see no more."

"So whadda ya wanna do?"

They both knew that neither of them wanted to go home.

"I wish we'd brought some lunch," said Dissun.

"If we'd tried they'd've know'd we was gonna sneak off. You know that."

"Yeah, but that don't mean I ain'tn't hungry."

They climbed down the tree and looked around, trying to pick the best way to go without risking being seen.

Dissun's stomach growled.

"Shush!" his brother said, holding up a hand and waving a palm.

"I can't help it. It's gots a mind of its own."

"No, not your stomach," said Dudderun. "I thinks I heard somethin'."

There was a rustle and this time both of the boys heard it. With the skills earned from several years of hiding from chores, they dropped to all fours and hugged the ground, listening.

34

"Which way'd it come from?" Dissun barely whispered.

Dudderun's face said *I can't tell.*

Like four-legged spiders, they crawled through the grass along the edge of the pond.

Whatever it was made another rustling sound.

"There it is again," said Dissun. "A susurration of sorts."

Dudderun nodded and motioned with his chin that they should crawl *that way.*

The rustling rustled and the boys crawled towards the noise. It rustled again. It rustled and rustled. And then it stopped.

And just when it stopped, the boys emerged into a clearing where the grass was smoothed flat underneath a huge shade tree. A hearty lunch rested on a large flat rock in the middle of it all.

Dissun started for the food, but his brother held him back.

"We don't know whose that is," Dudderun warned.

"Nope," Dissun wriggled free, "but it's ours now."

Dudderun looked around and saw nothing. So he shrugged and went to join his brother who was sitting on the rock and had already eaten half a loaf of bread and was preparing to stuff a chunk of cheese into his mouth.

Snap!

The net pulled tight around the boys and they were hoisted high into the air.

Dissun stopped eating.

"I told ya so!" Dudderun yelled, grabbing at the webbing of rope.

"No's you didn't!"

"Did so."

"You said we didn't know whose food it was. You didn't say nothin' about it bein' a trap."

"Same thing."

"Isn't!"

"What's that sound?" Dudderun looked around. "Sounds like… grunting."

"I told you not to put the rock in it!" a voice came from somewhere behind the tree.

"It looked nicer on a table-like," said another.

The voices were distinctly individual, but shared a low, croaky gargle in their intonations.

"Seelies?" Dissun whispered to his brother.

"More likely *un*seelies," his brother answered. "Seelies don't do this kinda thing."

"Shut up the both of ya!" growled one of their captors. "We's got work to do and don't want to hear nunna yer whinin'."

"We wasn't whinin'," said Dudderun. "We was just wondering what you are."

"Why…." said one of the voices, trying to sound sweet, "we're the Gwragedd Annwn." Croaking giggles bobbled from behind the trunk of the tree.

"What's a Gwerdiggity Annawanna?" Dissun whispered to his brother.

"You know!" Dudderun whispered back. "Them's the fairies what live under the lake that grandpa always talks about in his sleep."

Dissun peered through the ropes. "Naw, I don't think so. They's supposed to be pretty."

"Only because they get to live by the lake!" a definitely not-giggling voice shouted back.

"C'mon," said Dudderun, "we can tell you're unseelies. You might as well show yourselves."

"We don't like that name."

"Well, if you don't come out, we can't figure out a different name for you, can we?"

There was some tittering behind the tree, and then a dozen little fairies stepped out into the clearing. They were about as tall as the tine of a pitchfork and just as skinny, with skinny legs sticking out from under tunics that looked like they were made of old sheets. They had equally skinny arms ending in hands as big as their feet and fingers as long as their toes. And each set of hands was straining to hold the end of a rope that was draped across the overhead branch and attached to the net that held the boys.

"So….," Dudderun looked at the unseelies, "what else do you want to be called?"

Both of the boys remembered the admonishments from their grandmother to always be polite to a fairy, seelie or unseelie.

"We don't know what else to answer to," said one with tangled green hair that hung to the knees. It stood in front of the others, who also had tangled green hair that hung to the knees.

Dissun thought for a moment. "How about if we say it politely? Like…," he gathered his best excuse-me-mum voice and said, "Unseelie."

The unseelies looked at each other, chattered a bit, then turned and nodded as one. The one in front, with the tangled green hair down to the knees, said, "That would be fine."

"So," an unseelie said to the others, "what are we going to do? It's too heavy to carry all that way."

"I told ya not to put that rock in there!"

"Yes. We already heard you."

"Ya should've listened."

"Yes. Now shut up and let's figure out what to do."

"We could drop it," said a tiny, but still croaky, voice. "Lift it up and drop it. Do it a buncha times 'till the rock breaks up and falls outta the net."

This was answered with a group of nodding green-haired heads.

"No!"

The nodding stopped and twenty-four unseelie eyes looked up at the boys.

Dudderun gathered himself and cleared his throat. "I'm sorry," he said, "but you can't do that."

"Why not?"

"Well, for one thing, you might kill us. Me and my brother, that is."

"He's got a point," said a green-haired unseelie. "We can't's hand 'em over if they's dead."

"We'd give it a listen if you've got any ideas," said one of the unseelies.

Dissun looked at his brother. They both had grins that were mildly frightening now that they had teeth behind them.

"You could open the net and we'll push the rock out," said Dissun.

"That might work," said an unseelie.

"Are you daft?" said another. "The minute we open the net they'll run off!"

The first unseelie looked back at the boys. "You ain't gonna run off, are you?"

Both boys held up their hands, palms forward. "We absolutely promise," they said in unison, having had years of practice doing the very same thing for their mother.

Dissun handed a hunk of cheese to his brother and they ate while the unseelies debated what to do. They were just finishing up when the unseelie in front, the one with the tangled green hair down to the knees, stepped up to the net.

"We're holdin' you to your promise," it said.

The boys nodded.

The unseelie bobbed its head at the others and they all let loose of their ropes.

Dissun and Dudderun scrambled over the rock, wriggled out of the net and ran as fast as they could towards the pond.

"You promised!" the unseelie shrieked from behind them.

"That's right," Dissun called back, laughing. "But we didn't say *what* we were promisin'."

"Not technically," laughed Dudderun.

"Breakin' promises is rude!" the unseelie yelled at them.

Dissun and Dudderun, still running as fast as their young legs could carry them, looked at each other. One was about to ask the other if they should be concerned when they fell flat on their faces and found themselves being dragged — pulled by long, tangled green hair that wrapped around their legs and feet — back to the huge tree where they'd first been caught.

"Well, it was worth a try," said Dissun.

"Still better than a day of shearing sheep," said Dudderun. His brother nodded.

Six

"What's that smell?" Dissun wrinkled his nose.

"I think they're cookin' stew," said Dudderin.

"That don't smell like no stew *I've* ever smelled."

They looked at the cage they'd been tossed into after being shoved back into the net, then dragged across the river and a field to the edge of the woods. On the wall behind them was a slab of wood with what looked like writing that had been hastily wiped over. To the side of them was a firepit with a large cauldron hanging on a hook and full of something that smelled as ripe as the worst of the days with their grandfather.

"It's goblin stew," came a low voice from somewhere across the cave. "Your people don't make stew like goblins do."

"Why does all of this seem familiar?" Dissun said to himself, but also to his brother.

"What happened to the Unseelies?" asked Dudderun

"Oh, they've got what they bartered for," said the goblin.

"And what was that," said Dudderun, "if you don't mind me askin'?"

"That I eat you instead of them."

"Ah," said Dudderun. He sat down next to his brother. "Well," he said, "this is new for us."

"It is," said Dissun, "but it's also not. I think I know where we've heard about this before. Hold on a minute," he said. Then he called out to the likho sitting against the far wall. "Not meaning to be nosey, you see," he said, "but are you, by any chance, blind?"

The likho grumbled a mirthless laugh. "Why do you ask?"

Dissun thought for a moment. Then he said, "We've heard stories about you. You're famous, you know."

It dawned on Dudderun where and with whom they were. "He's right. We've been hearin' tales about you since we was babies."

The twins looked at each other and grinned. *We've got this one figured out*, they nodded.

"I'm sure you have," growled the likho. "It wasn't a random thing, those unseelies catching the two of you."

The twins lost their grins.

"I've smelled you two since your mother was in that cage. She's the reason I've been blind for the past ten years." The likho rose from where it was sitting in the shadowed recess of the cave. "I figure she owes me one." It thought of what it'd just said, then laughed, "or two!"

"In the stories she told, our mum said you had family," said Dudderun, looking around the room, trying to find clues towards an escape.

"I did. But they couldn't stand to be with me after I tore my eyes out." The likho sighed. "Weak and no good at being careful, that's what they said I was." The tree-goblin almost sounded pathetic, but it caught itself. "Bah! Who needs them?" The likho paused, scratched its head just above an empty eye socket.

Deciding to ignore those concerns for the moment, the likho found the cauldron, dipped a hand in the bubbling broth and stirred. It stuck a long finger in its mouth. "Mmmm…," it said, smacking its non-existent lips. "*Nummy!*"

44

Trying for a diversion away from any conversation regarding them being served as stew, Dissun piped up and asked, "Where's your eyes?"

The likho turned on them, scarred sockets where flashing eyes would have been, and snarled, "Brainless hobgoblins!" A heavy fist slammed on the wall, rattling the rock. Little stones fell on its head.

Dissun and Dudderun watched the pebbles fall.

"Oh yeah, I remember now," said Dudderun. "The old goblin lady grabbed 'em up and carried them off in her little pouch."

The likho remembered clearly the events of that day, and said, "I'll be getting those wretched hobgoblins next. Right after I'm done digesting you."

"I dunno know about that," said Dudderun, choosing to ignore that last bit from the likho, "I hear they're pretty smart, those hobgoblins."

"Rrrrraaarrwwrrrruuugggghhhrrrrr…!!!" the likho roared. "Not smarter than me! I have *rings* of wisdom in my trunk, and even the smallest leaf on my smallest twig could outwit one of them."

"And stronger," said Dissun."

"Those weak little things?" the likho scoffed.

"Oh, yes," said Dissun. "There's lots of stories about them," he paused for effect, then added, "more stories about them than there are about you, even."

The likho roared and slammed its fist against the cave wall again. More pebbles fell on its head.

The boys looked at each other, and they dove into a barrage of annoyance unlike anything the tree-goblin had encountered before. They needled and wheedled, making it angrier with every question and comment. And the likho growled and roared. It stomped and slammed its fists against the walls of the cave. With each smash, rocks fell on its head. At first, small pebbles and stones. Then larger rocks. Until, with a final massive blow, the sides of the cave filled with cracks and the entire thing came crashing down.

Dissun and Dudderun grabbed the slab of wood from the wall behind them and held it above their heads, shielding themselves from the deluge of crumbled cave. When it was over, the cage around them was nothing but broken twigs and they easily stepped out of their prison.

Dissun looked over his shoulder towards the rubble as they found a path that might take them home. "D'ya think he's dead?"

"Dunno," said Dudderun.

They walked a bit more, then Dudderun put his hand on his brother's shoulder.

"Slow down," he said.

"Why?"

"We don't wanna make it home 'til after its dark and them sheep is all done bein' sheared."

Seven

*D*issun and Dudderun strolled down the dirt path towards the pond, each holding a stick across one shoulder, and each stick with a bag tied to the end that bobbed up and down as they walked. Large wicker baskets were carried in their other hands.

"How many fish d'ya figure we have to catch before we can go back?" asked Dissun.

"I dunno," answered Dudderun. "How many d'ya think would make up for skippin' the shearing? And then how many more would we need that might make mum happy so's we can get back to sleepin' in our own beds? That straw in the barn is okay, but them goats is makin' me *all* itchy."

"Everybody was pretty upset about it. I'm thinking maybe we'll be needin' twice as much as whatever we think it is."

Dudderun groaned, "We should've left earlier if we wanted to catch *that* many."

"Yeah," said Dissun, "but you know our mum wouldn't let us go without packin' us a lunch. Even if she *is* annoyed with us."

"I don't think *annoyed* is the right word for it."

"Well, we're not allowed to say any of the words grandpa was usin'," said Dissun. He pointed towards the pond. "Let's go sit over there," he said, "I think I seen fishes swimmin' 'round in that spot before."

The two brothers found a rock that looked fairly comfortable for sitting, set their sticks down and untied the bags of lunch.

"What's this?" Dudderun held up a jug.

"Goat milk," said Dissun.

"I don't think I want nothin' to do with goats. I didn't knows how disgustin'ly dirty they was 'til after sleepin' in their pen." Dudderun reached back to scratch his rump.

Dissun opened the jug, took a sip, and scrunched his face like a corkscrew. "Tastes about as good as they smell." He stuck his tongue out, as if giving it air might make the sour disappear. "This must've been from one of the older goats."

"Yep," said Dudderun, "our mum's mad at us, alright."

They decided to drink water from the pond instead, and set about tying string to the sticks, and tying hooks to the string, and looking for worms to poke the hooks through.

Dissun stopped. He held up a hand. "Sshhh…."

"What?"

"I heard a susurration. Like the one we's heard before."

"Unseelies!"

The twin boys looked around. The last time they'd heard the grass rustling like that, they'd found themselves caught up in a net and turned over to the likho goblin for its stew.

"Come on out," said Dissun. He wanted to add a few choice words and a couple of colorful names, but remembered that you must always be polite to a fairy – even the unseelies.

"But don't be tryin' nothin'," Dudderun chimed in. "We're on to you and your sneakin' ways."

"Sneaking?" An unseelie, stepped out from behind a copse of tall grass. "We didn't do no sneakin'. We was just fulfillin' a barter."

"Yeah, a barter for the likho to eat us instead've you."

"It seemed a fair deal to us," said the unseelie, "and you're still alive. So it appears it's all worked out finely."

Unable to argue with that logic, Dissun and Dudderun relaxed a bit.

"Well, come on out, all of you." Dissun gestured towards the knee-high grass that hadn't stopped susurrating. "We knows there's more of ya."

Eleven more unseelies stepped out from the grass.

"So…," said the first unseelie, "ya goin' fishin'?"

"Uh-huh," said Dudderun, his fingers back to digging in the dirt for worms.

"What's that ya gots there?" The unseelie pointed at the jug.

"Old goat milk," said Dissun. "The milk's not old. It's the goat that's long in the tooth."

The unseelies glanced sideways at one another, tittering.

Dissun and Dudderun pulled their fingers from the mud and grinned at each other. They'd heard stories about certain kinds of fairies having a strong affinity towards goat's milk, and were sensing an opportunity for something that might work to their advantage.

"You know," said Dudderun, "I'm thinking maybe we should have an early lunch, just so's we can get to that goat milk all the sooner."

"I know what you mean," Dissun rubbed his belly, "I can't hardly waits for it."

Dudderun reached for the jug and opened it. He took a long, dramatic sniff, and turned his head to hide the green his face was turning.

The tittering among the unseelies reached a buzzing, and the first one stepped forward. It cleared its skinny throat. "Ahem... I don't suppose you'd be willing to share?"

"Oh, we'd like to." Dissun did the talking until Dudderun was able to contain the bile and force it back to his gullet where it belonged. "But we love it so much. We're not sure we can part with it."

Dudderin held the jug aloft, making motions as if to bring it to his mouth for a big swallow. Very slow motions, so as to give the unseelies time to interrupt.

"What if we were to barter something for it?"

"What could possibly be as good as goat milk?" Dissun held the jug aloft as if it was a trophy, and to put some distance between the aroma and his nose.

"Well...," the first unseelie looked around and spied the wicker baskets. "You're here to catch some fish?"

"Yep," said Dudderun. "We gots to bring back these two baskets full on account of you's stealing us away from helpin' with the shearing."

Dissun nodded.

"With those sticks and hooks?"

"That's how it's done," said Dissun.

"We can catch the fish much easier than that," said the unseelie. "Could save you a lot of time." It looked back at the eleven others standing behind, nodding enthusiastically. "That would be the barter. Fish for milk."

Dissun and Dudderun looked at each other, at the baskets and jugs of sour milk, then at each other again.

Dudderun started to put his hand out to shake on it when Dissun grabbed his wrist.

Dissun squinted at the unseelie and asked, "How many fish?"

"You'll have fish in both your baskets."

"That's not really an answer," said Dudderun.

"One drink for one fish," said Dissun.

The unseelies huddled together, then turned and every one of them nodded. The first unseelie held its hand out to shake.

"And we get to pick the cup for drinkin' out of," said Dissun, holding his hand back.

Now the first unseelie was the one to squint. "And we pick the fish."

Thinking they'd better not push it any further, the boys agreed, and hands were shook.

The unseelies took up positions, sitting along the rocks at the edge of the pond. Eleven of them waited while the first dipped its long, green, scraggly hair down into the water, swishing it around. It didn't take a minute before a fish took a nibble and found itself tangled, wrapped up in the long hairs, and pulled out of the water.

The unseelie reached out, its long fingers grasping in the air. "Milk," it said.

Dudderun took the cork from one of the jugs and dug a hole into it to make it into a cup. He poured in some milk, gave it to the unseelie, and took possession of the fish.

The unseelie drank the milk, then turned and nodded to the rest of the fairies, smacking its skinny lips. Nodding back, they all dropped their hair into the water and commenced to catching fish while Dissun and Dudderun dug in their pockets for other things that might serve as fairy-sized drinking vessels.

Pretty soon the baskets were overflowing with fish, the jugs were empty of goat milk, and the unseelies were laughing and chattering and falling off the rocks.

"They's actin' like grandpa does when he gets into those barrels at the back of the barn," said Dissun as he tried to tie the lid shut on the overstuffed basket.

"I'd bet they'll be wantin' some more," said Dudderun. "A couple more days of this and maybe our mum will forget some of the other stuff we done, too."

The boys proposed the idea of meeting again tomorrow and doing it all over again.

"As long as it's the same goat," said the first unseelie.

Eight

The next afternoon, Dissun and Dudderun lounged under a nearby tree while the unseelies happily caught fish and drank goat milk, chattering away as they did.

"Them Unseelies," Dissun said to his brother, "they's sure do chatter a lot."

"What're they talkin' about?"

"I dunno."

"Shhh! Let's listen."

"Well, I think it's all her own fault," said one unseelie. The boys couldn't tell which one, but it didn't really matter.

"How's that?" said another.

"You've seen how she carries that bag. Swingin' it around. Droppin' it in the mud and water. It's no wonder everything's all squishy inside."

"I dunno. Them likho eyes was certainly cursed. Stick 'em inna bag with hobgoblin eyes and of course that curse is gonna spread."

"He tore thems out before they was cursed."

"You sure about that?"

"That all don't matter. That young hobgoblin girl don't pay no attention."

"Well, I guess we'll find out tonight what they plan on doin'."

"Shhh! Them boys're listenin'!"

All twelve unseelies shut up and looked at the boys. One of the unseelies burped.

"What's goin' on tonight?" asked Dissun.

"Can't tells ya."

"Aw, c'mon," said Dudderun. "We gave you all that milk."

"And we gave you all them fishes's's," said an unseelie who had drunk more milk than it should have.

"We can get more milk," Dissun offered.

"When?"

"Tomorrow," said Dudderun.

"Too late. The thing's tonight."

"Shhh! Don't tells 'em that!"

"Tell you what," said Dissun, "we go home and after supper we sneaks out and bring you some more."

"And you tell us what's goin' on," said Dudderun.

"And you take us there," Dissun added, looking at his brother with a slight *why not try?* shrug.

"More milk!" sang the chorus of unseelies.

"Be here before the moon rises," said the first unseelie. "We'll have a bit of a way to walk, and we gots ta be there afore the moon starts to shine on the meadow."

Dissun and Dudderun nodded.

The unseelies disappeared into the grass, disturbing the grasshoppers and field-mice with their chanting of "Goat milk! Goat milk!"

From behind the bushes, Dissun and Dudderun watched the moon rise over the meadow and, as it rose, small dark shapes of all different sizes shuffled in the grass, making their way towards the tall, dead tree in the middle of the field.

"Goblins!" whispered Dissun.

"Shh!" An unseelie hushed them. "Goblins can hear better'n anything."

"That tree looks familiar," said Dudderun.

"Shh!" The unseelie hushed them again. "That's the likho."

"It's lookin' kinda crumpled," Dissun snickered.

The unseelie nodded to the eleven other unseelies and, not wanting to be there when the boys got caught by goblins with good ears, they took their jug of milk and snuck away to another bush.

When most of the goblins had reached the long feet of the dead tree, it straightened as well as it could and began to speak.

"Goblins," said the likho, "that you came here shows how much you agree with me."

"Not really," a goblin called out. "Most of us just didn't have much else to do."

A wave of laughter rolled through the gathering.

"And we heard there's to be snacks after," said another. Goblin heads nodded.

"There's nothing been said about snacks," the likho replied.

A murmuring wave of reckoning and finger-pointing at who'd begun the rumor washed over the congregation.

The likho clenched its barked jaw. *This* was why nobody wanted to associate with hobgoblins. But, for its plan to work, the inanity would have to be tolerated.

The likho raised its voice just a bit. "The humans are a curse that must be eradicated."

"Them's some big words, likho," cackled a hobgoblin.

"The humans have to go!" The likho used its best authoritative voice.

"Why?"

"They ruined my home!"

"Seems you brought that on yerself," said a goblin somewhere in the middle of the crowd.

"And that's why you's all crumpled up!" called out another.

"It's because of them that I am blind," growled the likho.

"Didn't you rip out yer own eyes?"

"Yeah, and then Edwina over there," the goblin pointed, disregarding that the likho couldn't see what it was pointing at, "she scooped 'em up and stuck 'em in her bag."

The likho couldn't tell which goblin was talking, having only sockets where its eyes should be. *Doesn't matter*, it thought, *they're all the same.*

"Edwina did what a goblin does," said the likho with disingenuous civility. "But it was the human woman that wrote words! And my eyes were cursed because of it. Most of you would've done the same thing." The likho paused, then said, "In fact, half of you rip out your own eyes for less than that."

"*That* is a tradition," a hobgoblin yelled. "Not the same thing."

"It's close," the likho parried.

"Isn't."

"You're still blind afterwards, aren't you?"

"But for different reasons, and that's what counts."

"Yeah," called out another goblin, "tradition says the females gotsta pull out their eyes an' put 'em inna bag for their daughters. It's always been thataway."

The likho noticed he was only hearing male goblin voices arguing about the difference between tearing out one's own eyes because of a curse versus doing it because of a tradition, and that tradition was acceptable while being cursed was questionable.

"Well, there was a curse on mine," the likho tried to steer things back to the plan. "And, odd as it may be, I didn't mind Edwina taking mine to save her own."

"Didn't seem you had much choice," a goblin cackled.

"Didn't you put a curse on her for it?" came another voice. "Sure seems like you minded it at the time."

"She broke tradition!" squawked the voice of a goblin that was distinctively male.

"Never you mind that!" Edwina shouted back. She sat next to her pig within hearing distance of the likho, but no closer than that. Having been caught up by this same likho once before, she didn't want to give it a second chance at having her for dinner. Neither as a guest, nor as the main course. In addition, although she was sure the curse had been meant for the unborn child carried by the woman, she wasn't exactly positive about it. The pig scooted closer to Edwina so the goblin could scratch between its ears with her long, ragged fingernails.

"And now," the likho continued its efforts to stay in charge, "you've all seen what happened to the bag of eyes."

"That's b'cause of your curse, you daft old piece of wood."

"It's because of the humans," the likho said.

"Tell them it's the curse, Daddy!" Mildred, seated next to her mother, cried to her father. Mildred had received the bag of goblins' eyes on her birthday and since then had carried it with her everywhere she went. She did what was her best to keep it like a goblin should. Unfortunately for the bag, her best was fairly substandard. Sometimes she dropped it. Sometimes she kicked it across the mud as she tried to pick it up. There was the time a cow rolled on it. Geese liked snatching it from her belt. However, rather than admit her own deficiencies, she chose to embrace the idea that the curse was upon the bag of eyes, regardless of what her mother said.

"That ain't no curse!" shouted a goblin who felt the need to chime in. "It's because she don't take care of it."

"Quit pickin' on my daughter," shouted Morris, who was seated next to Mildred. Although Morris was Edwina's husband and Mildred's father, in the arrangement of this particular goblin family hierarchy, he wasn't much more relevant than that. He didn't know whether the curse was upon the bag of eyes or the woman's offspring, but he was smart enough to keep any thoughts upon the subject to himself, and to use the opportunity to defend his daughter.

"Irregardless!" boomed the likho.

"That ain't a word," a hobgoblin from somewhere in the back yelled out. It was rewarded with a great deal of cackling.

"The humans need to go," said the likho.

Hobgoblins, while not particularly liking anyone else, including other goblins, had a special place in their loathing hearts for humans. Other than the gold and silver, and the occasional tasty infant, what use were they?

To the boys, who'd crept closer to hear, the nodding heads and murmuring of agreement amongst the horde of goblins meant something was afoot that didn't bode well for their own human kind, and maybe it was time for them to get involved.

Dissun cleared his throat and dug down deep in the guttural. "How's about if we gets the old hags some new eyes?" He'd heard his grandfather refer to female goblins as hags and, seeing no strong reaction, figured he hadn't mischosen his words.

A couple of goblins in the back row looked around and shrugged *wasn't me* to each other.

Half of the goblins, the female half, were muttering amongst themselves.

"Can we do that?" It was an old blind hag, empty sockets where her eyes once were, who said this.

"Nobody ever told us that's was an option," said another old hag, who was also blind, with empty eye sockets.

"Wait a minute!" yelled the likho, waving its branch-like arms around. "This isn't about replacing eyes. It's about driving out the humans."

"I'd be bettin' you'd like a new pair of eyes, too," yet another old hag said to the likho. This one's sockets had been empty for a great number of years longer than most of the others'.

The likho didn't say anything else. And, after a moment of thinking, realized the old goblin was right. He *would* like to be able to see again. *Then* he could drive out the humans by himself without any wretched hobgoblins messing things up.

Meanwhile, as the female goblins argued with the male goblins regarding the necessity of vision and whether the male goblins would like to be blundered over their heads by female goblins holding very large clubs, Dudderun and Dissun whispered to each other.

"How're they gonna get new eyes?"

"I dunno. But we'd better figure somethin' out or our mum's gonna be pretty angry when she sees a buncha goblins comin' over the hill to drive us all out."

"She'd fight them."

"I know."

"And then we'd be stuck cleaning up after a buncha goblins lumped all over the ground."

"I know."

"We'd better figure somethin' out."

"Yep."

"What about the Unseelies?" said Dudderun. "Don't fairies give out magic-type favors?"

"You need to see a seelie for that," said the unseelie in front of the other eleven. Seeing a potential opportunity for more goat milk, they were coming back over to the boys.

"And if we give you some more goat milk you can tell us where to find one?" asked Dissun. He was pretty much sure he was figuring the unseelies out.

"A jug for us," said the unseelie, "and you'll need some more milk for the seelie. Fairies don't just hand out favors for free."

"Isn't that what a favor is?" asked Dissun. "A favor is somethin' ya do as…," he tried to think of another word, "…a favor-like."

"Otherwise it's a barter," said Dudderun.

"Oh, you don't want to be barterin' with a seelie," said the unseelie, "they's tricky buggers and you'll end up bein' very sorry for tryin'."

The boys made the deal with the unseelies and agreed to meet back at the pond at midnight, which was the time in which seelies came out for a swim, according to the unseelies.

Before they left, Dissun found his guttural again and called out over the shrub, "Come back tomorrow and you'll get some new eyes."

Since the goblins didn't know where the voice was coming from, they couldn't tell whether to pay it any mind or not. But half of them were tired of hearing the females complaining about having to give up their eyes, and the other half were tired of hearing about tradition, so they decided to agree the mystery voice didn't sound as corrupted as most and they all went home, a good number of them muttering about having to congregate a second time.

"Why'd you offer new eyes anyhow?" asked Dudderun as they headed home.

"Don't rightly know. It just popped into my brain. I mean, after all of mum's stories haven't you always wondered how them old hags felt about it all?"

"Yeah, but I dunno. How's we gonna do that?"

Dissun shrugged. "My brain ain't quite got that far."

"Well," said Dudderun, "midnight's not far away. Let's hope either your brain or mine comes up with somethin'."

Nine

*T*he unseelies made good on their promise and, right around midnight, they stood by as the boys approached a seelie just as it was jumping into the pond for a swim. Just as they'd never seen an unseelie prior to a couple of days ago, the boys had never seen a seelie either. It was interesting, the twins thought, how two things can be so similar and so different at the same time. The seelie managed to accomplish those differences with a much preferable quality.

The seelie was about the same size as the unseelies, but where unseelies appeared skinny the seelie was thin. Unseelies wore a tunic that looked like an old bedsheet and the seelie wore a tunic that looked like bedlinen. Both had long green hair, but while the unseelies' hung in a tangle to the knees, the seelie's gently floated on an invisible breeze. The large hands and feet at the ends of long legs and arms were not dissimilar, except that the seelie's just, somehow, seemed more delicate.

After a moment of looking between the two versions of fairy, the boys shook their heads and got down to business. They told the seelie what they needed and the seelie happily accepted the jug of goat milk as a gift, not a barter, for the favor.

The next night Dissun and Dudderun hid behind the same shrub as they'd been the night before. They didn't need the unseelies to show them the way, but the fairies had come along to watch.

Hobgoblins surrounded the likho. To one side was a gaggle of old blind females chattering about the last thing they'd seen – mostly their own hands – and to the other side was a collection of old not-blind male goblins standing with their arms crossed and grumbling about tradition. In the middle were all the other goblins, some watching to see what was going to happen, others pondering if they could somehow profit from the event, and several carrying empty sacks in the hopes that there might be gold or silver or infants involved.

The boys had considered leaving a note tied to a rock as a means of telling the goblins what they had to do in order to get their new eyes. However, they realized that would result in every goblin in the field tearing its eyes out and, as entertaining as that might be to watch, their preference was not to cause any harm to the things. Besides, they didn't want to waste the favor the seelie had granted them.

"Waahhh...." cried Dissun, doing his best to imitate a baby.

"Boo-hoo," said Dudderun.

"Baby's don't say boo-hoo," whispered Dissun.

Dudderun nodded and mimicked his brother with a loud wail. "Waaahhhh!"

Every goblin head turned toward the sounds.

"What's that?"

"An infant?"

"What's an infant doin' out here? And at night, no less."

"Don't matter. I'm gonna eat it!"

"Not if I get to it first!"

Dissun and Dudderun hadn't grasped how fast a goblin can run when its intended catch is a juicy young baby. The boys sprinted faster than they'd ever gone before, wailing and crying as they ran. The unseelies ran with them, not that they feared the goblins but because they didn't want to miss out on the fun when either the boys were caught, or they made it back to the pond where their plan would be seen through.

Reaching the pond with the goblins uncomfortably close on their heels, the boys jumped into the water and swam out to the middle.

Goblins smacked into each other when the first ones reached the water's edge. Goblins don't usually swim as water tends to remove all the well-earned detritus and aroma from the body. Besides, the crying had stopped.

"Where's the infant?" one of them sniffed the air.

"Maybe it's in the pond."

"Babies don't swim."

"I didn't say it was swimmin'."

The debate continued for a few minutes, until it was interrupted by a croak and a splash.

"Was that a frog?"

"Sounded like a big 'un."

"Frogs ain't infants, but they's good anyhow!"

"Ladies first!" yelled one of the old blind hags. She dove into the water, rummaged around, emerged with a large frog and stuffed it in her mouth.

With hoots and hollers, all the other goblins did the same. Even the likho reached down with its long branches and snatched frogs from the water.

"They's greedy, ain't they?" said Dissun.

"We didn't take that into account when that seelie put the charm on the croakers."

"Yeah."

The boys watched the melee.

"This is even better'n we expected," said Dudderun.

"Yeah."

When the sun rose the next morning, the goblins, scattered along the edges of the pond where they'd fallen asleep with overstuffed bellies, moaned and groaned as they regained consciousness. The sounds of awakening turned to cries of joy when formerly blind goblins found they'd regained their sight, then it turned to curses when they learned they'd gained more sight than they'd ever had before. The seelie's charm had been that, for every charmed frog a goblin ate, they'd win two eyes. Two frog eyes.

And since they were greedy, most of the goblins had eaten several frogs.

And since most heads only have sockets for one pair of eyes, the extra frog eyes popped out anywhere else they could find room on the wrinkled skin that loosely covered the hobgoblin head.

The goblins groaned and complained, wobbling around in unintentional directions. When they bumped into each other they attempted at an argument, but since there were eyeballs on every side of their heads, and because not all of the eyeballs were set in the way that would allow them to see straight and upright, the goblins had trouble finding with whom they were arguing.

Eventually they gave up and went home.

"Pile that straw up a little higher," Dissun stood back and instructed his brother.

"Is that good?" asked Dudderun.

"It's very good on this side," said an unseelie, sticking its head over the top of the small mound Dudderun had created. "It'll do."

Dudderun climbed down from the loft and the two boys assessed their work.

"So," said Dudderun, "all's we gotta do is let them stay up there and give them some goat milk every day…"

"And they'll keep us up on our chores," Dissun finished.

"You sure nobody's gonna find out?"

"Hope not."

"Not even mom?"

"Hope not even more."

Ten

*E*dwina rode the pink pig, her goblin mind deep in hobgoblin thought. She was grumpy and grumbling. Being a goblin, she was always grumpy and grumbling, but today she was grumpy and grumbling more than usual.

Her red cap slipped to one side, revealing a pair of frog-eyes just above her ear. The little bird riding on her shoulder grabbed the cap with its beak, tucking it back in place.

The magpie, digging its tiny talons in the goblin's shoulder was one reason she was grumpy. The red cap refusing to stay in place was another.

The dozen or so sets of frog-eyes all around her head – some stretched among the straggly hairs, others peeking out from between the folds of her speckled scalp, some upright, some sideways, others upside down – those were the principal cause of her grumpiness and grumblingness.

As if having eyeballs popping up all over the head wasn't bad enough, getting the brain to figure out which ones to look out of was worse. Ever since the smorgasbord of frogs at the pond, goblins were stumbling in all directions. More than a few of them had been squished underneath the also-stumbling likho. Edwina noted that those were mostly male goblins who were adamantly fond of tradition, and had eaten the charmed toads even though they weren't missing any of their own eyes, and she felt not so bad about the squishing. But she was pretty sure one of the squished old females might have been a great-great-grandmother or something and for that she felt a tiny wiggle of melancholy deep in her belly. Not in her heart, though. Goblin hearts weren't for feelings. That's what guts and bellys were for.

Morris and Mildred, Edwina's husband and daughter and two of the few goblins who hadn't feasted on the pond frogs, had gathered together an assortment of old caps, sewn them together, and made something that could cover all the extra eyes so their wife and mother could amble about without falling over so much.

Yes, having more eyes than the pair you were meant to be using at a time would make any goblin irritable. And Edwina had the distinction of being able to broaden any circumstances into an occasion for a cantankerousness beyond the likes of what most have ever seen. And she wasn't going to let the small detail of her family trying to adjust her discomfort change how she felt.

Those were the reasons for her grumping and grumbling, but they were not why her hobgoblin mind was deep in thought.

The reason for her deep goblin thoughts was the *cause* of the excess eyes.

"Maybe you should just tie a scarf over it all," suggested the magpie.

"Goblins wear red caps, not scarfs!" Edwina snapped. She was in no mood for suggestions. "Find a wart or something to tuck it around."

Try as they might have, Morris and Mildred were neither tailor nor seamstress, and the fenagled cap was wide in one place, tall in another, and snug in nowhere at all.

The bird attempted what Edwina proposed, but the mole was so big it only made the cap pull off the wart on the other side.

"Blast you, bird! Can't you do anything right?"

"Wock!" said the magpie, "I'm only trying to help. You could try to appreciate that a little bit." It flitted up and over to the other shoulder, and pulled the cap back over the hair-sprouting wart.

Edwina snorted, but said no more. For the time being.

The pig was tired after carrying the hobgoblin from the cave to the pond, and shook its pink hide in joyful relief when Edwina finally dismounted at the water's edge. The goblin didn't need to look to the night sky to know it was almost midnight.

"Stay and keep an eye on the pig," she instructed the magpie as she adjusted the burlap sack hanging on her belt. It was bigger than the bag of eyes she used to carry and she hadn't yet acclimated to it swinging around and down to her feet.

"Fine with me," said the bird. Magpies are not night birds and picking bugs from the pig's back was a much favored alternative to whatever it was the goblin intended to do down at the pond. The bird had learned this from experience. "But if you find something shiny, be a dear and bring it back for me."

"Yeah, yeah…" Edwina crouched. She didn't need to. Goblins aren't much taller than switchgrass, and she was of average height for a goblin. But crouching set the mood. She hunkered down and snuck through the bushes to the water's edge. And she saw, sitting on a mossy rock just a little ways away, the seelie she was looking for.

Keeping her eye on the fairy, Edwina pulled a net from the sack. Her goblin mouth stretched into a sneer, with yellowed teeth jagging out in odd directions, and her eyes — the original, goblin ones — squinted as they focused on their quarry. She waited until the fairy looked down to dip its little fairy fingers in the pond, and —

"Gotcha!" Edwina jumped and threw the net over the seelie.

The seelie didn't struggle, which was a bit of a let-down for the goblin. Instead it looked through the netting and sighed.

"I was expecting someone like you," said the seelie.

"You was?" Edwina was surprised, then remembered herself and said it again with more antagonism. "You was!" That didn't sound right either, so she didn't say anything else and let the seelie explain what it meant.

"Well, maybe not exactly you," said the seelie. "It was only supposed to be the goblin hags that got themselves a new pair of eyes," the seelie said. "But that goat milk hindered the quality of the charm. And you goblins — I'd forgotten how greedy you all are."

"So you admit it?" Edwina felt slightly discouraged. She wanted this to be a moment of triumph, and the quick admission of guilt was almost as disheartening as the lack of struggle on the part of the fairy.

"Of course I do. There's nobody else who could do a charm like that, is there?"

Edwina wasn't sure of that. There could be other seelies, maybe even an unseelie or two, with that kind of skill. But there didn't seem to be a point in arguing. Besides, she sensed there was something more to the story.

"Why'd you make the charm, then?"

"Well," said the fairy, "like I said, it wasn't supposed to go like it did. It was the goat milk that got me out of sorts."

"Goat milk?" Edwina's brain skittered towards a variety of possibilities.

"Those boys."

Edwina's brain stopped skittering and squatted in place.

"They gifted goat milk for the charm. Said it was to save their family."

"How did they know...?" Edwina mumbled.

"What?"

"Never mind. What did the boys do?"

"They said goblins were coming after their family, and it was because the old ones – the females – didn't have eyes. They gave me a jug of goat milk as a gift for a charm that would give the goblins the eyes of a frog."

"Uh-huh…."

"It was old goat milk!" The seelie's voice squeaked in anger and its delicately oversized hands curled into fists that thumped on the mossy stone.

"How old was the milk?"

"Not old milk. The goat was old. Probably the most ancient in the herd."

"So? What's that mean?"

"For a fairy, goat milk is the most delicious thing there is. But if the goat is old, it turns on us. Unseelies like the feeling. But we seelies, we're more respectable and don't participate in such things. Being under the influence of the milk of an old goat made the charm go all awry." The seelie cocked its head sideways and looked at Edwina. "And the greed within you goblins didn't help."

"How was we to know?"

"What? When to be greedy and when not to be greedy? You're greedy all the time."

"So's that just means *you* should'a known."

Edwina's intentions had been to snag the seelie and bring it back to the hobgoblins where it would meet its comeuppance, with the intended result of the hobgoblins quitting their blathering about how Mildred showed such wretched care for her bag of goblins' eyes. She realized comeuppance for the fairy wouldn't solve the additional eyeball problem, but it would make everyone feel better. The seelie wouldn't feel better, but that was neither here nor there.

However, now that she knew what she'd just learned, the goblin's craving for revenge changed its course. It was the boys who caused this. *Lousy, detestable doppelgangers!* she thought. *I'll butter 'em up and eat 'em on toast!*

Pulling herself into a position that might have appeared casual in any other creature, Edwina asked the seelie what could be done to correct the damage and assuage the ill attitudes of the goblins toward all seelies of the world.

The seelie, after insisting on being let out of the net first, told the goblin what was necessary.

Eleven

*D*issun and Dudderun snored in the straw-filled loft of the barn. They'd moved there and called it their bedroom shortly after the unseelies had moved in and their mother'd begun questioning their working hours.

The deal was made that, in exchange for the milk of the oldest goat on the farm, the unseelies would do all the work and complete all the chores that were expected of the boys. The problem was, when they slept in the house their mother knew when they were coming and going and, after a few days of not going until mid-afternoon, she started asking questions. So Dissun and Dudderun told her they could get to their chores much easier if they lived in the barn – right next to all the work that needed to get done.

"If'n we wakes up every morning to see all the work that's needin' doin'," they told her, "we won't forget any of it, and it'll all get done."

Their mother knew better than to believe them completely, but she considered how nice it would be to not have them underfoot, and she considered how all that really mattered to her was that the work and chores got done. She gave them her no-nevermind about it and they took their pillows and bedding and went to sleep in the barn.

As she approached the farm, Edwina knew exactly where the boys were. She could smell them. Not just because they hadn't bathed since the last rain, which had occurred two seasons prior, but because they smelled like human boys. No longer tasty-smelling like when they were infants, but distinctive nonetheless.

Glad that she'd left the magpie and pig back at the pond, she slunk across the farm field, between the stacks of wood and bags of grain, and into the barn. The point of her elongated nose quivered as she sniffed the air and followed the scent up the ladder and peered over the edge of the loft. *There they are,* she thought, *snuggled all comfy in their little blankies.* She suppressed a cackle.

With a burst of enthusiasm, she bounded up the last rung heaved herself at the sleeping boys.

"Hah!" she squealed with glee and released a well-timed fart as she landed on them.

"Ahah!" came a shout from behind her, and a few coughs when whoever said it caught her smelly odor.

Edwina, still squatting over the bundles underneath the blankets, turned her head. "Ack!" she shouted, and hopped around to face the two boys standing behind her holding pitchforks in their hands. Twelve unseelies crawled out from the bedding. The red cap on her head slid to one side revealing three extra sets of eyes that blinked in the straw-dust.

"What're ya doin' here?" Dissun menaced the goblin with his pitchfork.

"Who are you?" Dudderun asked, thinking he'd like to know a goblin name, also pointing his pitchfork.

"She cames to get ya," said an unseelie pulling its long, tangled green hair out from under a pillow.

"I wasn't doin' no such thing!" protested Edwina. "And my name's Edwina," she added, and curtsied as she'd heard proper folk do. "Might I have the pleasure of knowin' your name?"

"Don't fall for it," warned a second unseelie with long. "Never tell a goblin your name."

"Why not?" asked Dissun.

"Aww…," Edwina waved a boney hand, mole-encrusted skin flapping on her arms as she did so, "them's just old wives' tales."

"We've heard about wives' tales," said Dudderun. "Our mum said they're true – most of 'em, that is – especially when it comes to goblins." He waggled the pitchfork.

Edwina, eyeing the long tines on the boy's weapon, pulled her cap down over the extra, exposed eyes, so she could keep her thoughts straight.

"I always wondered," said Dissun, "is it the tales that are old, or the wives?"

"Probly both," said Dudderun. "Now, don't get all distracted. Keep to the situation at hand."

Dissun nodded and jabbed his pitchfork in Edwina's direction in order to let her know he wasn't distracted and was, in fact, attuned to the situation.

The goblin looked down and saw she was surrounded by unseelies. They were only as tall as her legs, and looked like they could quickly scramble given the need. She bided her time and hoped a beneficial moment might somehow arise.

"We know why she's here," said an unseelie.

Edwina looked down and counted only eleven at her feet. She wasn't fast enough to look up and see the twelfth swinging on a rope as it flew by and snatched the red cap off her head.

Dissun and Dudderun gasped.

"It's all yer fault!" wailed the goblin.

"You's didn't hafta eat so many toads!" It was an unseelie that said this.

"We're goblins. What'd ya think was gonna happen?"

The boys realized she had a point. They looked at one another, without the usual grins.

"So why'd you come here?" asked Dissun.

"She wants revenge!" another unseelie shrieked. It ran up and kicked the goblin in the shin.

"Ouch!" Edwina hopped on one leg, massaging the tiny spot where the unseelie's foot had made contact. "There's no need for that, is there?"

"Is they right?" asked Dudderun.

"Well...." Edwina hadn't thought the evening would come to her having to make an excuse, and she wasn't very adept at doing such things on-the-spot.

"Ahah!" Dissun yelled. "You want payback!"

Below them, a cow mooed and its bell rang as it shuffled in its stall.

"Shhh!" hissed Dudderun. "We's don't want nobody else comin' out here."

"Especially, not our mum," said Dissun.

"Yeah, *especially* not our mum."

Something clicked in Edwina's head. "Your mum?" she said. "Was your mum, by any chance, ever caught up by a likho goblin? Likes, maybe, a big goblin that looks like a tree?"

The boys looked at each other, their mouths drawing into gapes.

"It's her!" Dissun squealed.

"You was the one with her?" asked Dudderun.

"Well… I…" Edwina wasn't sure which way this was going to go, so she wasn't sure whether confirmation or denial was the best route.

"Hah!" laughed Dissun, looking aside at his brother and nodding his head towards the goblin. "We's friends."

"We are?" Edwina was confounded.

"Sure," said Dudderun putting aside his pitchfork and nodding at his brother to do the same. "You and our mum escaped the likho together. That makes you and her teammates."

"It does?" Edwina was a little less confounded, but still a bit befuddled.

"Sure does," said Dissun. "And then we was caught up by the same likho later on."

"Took him ten years to get to us," said Dudderun, "but he sure did. And we gots away, just like you and our mum did."

"How'd he catch you?" asked the goblin.

"We don't talk about that," chimed in an unseelie.

"Ah, it's okay," Dissun said. "The Unseelies bartered us to save themselves. But it all turned out okay, and now we're bunkmates." He gestured, indicating the loft.

"So," Edwina pointed at her many-eyed head, "why'd ya do this?" Her hobgoblin arm whipped into the air, snatching the cap from the still-swinging unseelie. "And gimme that back!" She plopped the cap back on her head, covering most of the eyes but being too stubborn to adjust it.

"We didn't mean to," said Dudderun. "Surely, we didn't."

"Them Unseelies took us to a gatherin' of goblins, and that likho – the one that looks like a tree – it'd got the buncha ya all riled up to try an' drive our family out."

"We didn't want to hafta be cleaning up a buncha goblins after they'd tried a'fightin' with our mum, so we figured we had to stops ya."

"Didn't work like you expected, did it?" said Edwina, pointing a long and rachety-nailed finger at her head for emphasis.

"Well, you goblins are all just so greedy."

"You knows that wasn't the only problem!" snapped the goblin.

"What? Why?"

"It was old goat milk," said Edwina.

The boys looked at each other. "We thought that's what fairies prefer," said Dissun.

"*Un*seelies prefer the milk from an old goat," Edwina snarled at the gaggle of fairies at her feet, restraining herself from an intestinal desire to kick at them. "Seelies got more refinement. They likes the stuff from a goat that ain't so timeworn."

The boys looked at the unseelies.

"Well, we didn't know *that*," said one of the skinny fairies.

"So, why'd you come here?" asked Dissun. "What was your plan?"

"Well," Edwina decided, considering the circumstances, she might try to be as honest as a goblin was capable of being. That capability not being one of their strong suits, she spoke quickly before it went away. "I was gonna capture you and feeds ya to whatever meanest thing I cames across first. And I was gonna get some young goat milk and take it to the seelie what's made that charm in the first place."

"Why're ya gonna do that?" asked Dissun.

"Because you need your comeuppances!"

"No. Why're ya gonna take the young milk to the fairy?" said Dudderun.

"It says it'll fix things if'n I do."

Unseelie eyes exchanged looks. "You can't trust a seelie," said one. "Did ya barter with it?"

"Of course I did," Edwina scoffed.

Dissun, Dudderun and twelve unseelies released a collective groan.

"What?" Edwina was feeling puzzled again.

"You can't barter with a seelie," said Dissun. "Ya gotsta ask 'em for a favor."

"And you give 'em somethin' for that favor."

"You're describing a barter," said Edwina.

"But, to the seelie, it's a *favor*. And you're just givin' it a gift for doin' it."

"Tell us exactly what the seelie asked for in exchange for puttin' things right," said the unseelie.

Edwina used a knotted thumb to count off the fingers on her oversized hand. "It's gonna fix a charm so's all the goblins'll go back to havin' just the two eyes."

"Uh-huh."

"I's to bring it summa that new goat milk.

"You mean the newest goat in the herd?"

"Of course."

"Okay. And…"

"And I's to bring it to the seelie tomorrow at midnight."

They all thought for a bit.

"By any chance," said Dudderun, "did the seelie tell ya how it wanted the milk delivered?"

Edwina thought for a moment. "No. It just said to brings it some new goat milk."

"It said it just like that?"

"Yes. Why?"

"Yeah," said Dissun, "why?"

"That seelie's gonna try'n trick you. Not sure how, but it's gonna do somethin' you'll not be expectin'. Fr'instance, you don't know if'n it might be wantin' the whole goat or just the milk from inside'a it." said Dudderun. "It didn't say the milk had to be *outta* the goat, did it? Like," he pointed at the unseelies, "*you* guys said to bring it in *jugs*."

"Them vexatious seelies!" snapped Edwina. The boys dodged the spittle flying from Edwina's yap.

Everyone thought for a bit more.

"I see another potential, too," said Dissun. "That seelie didn't say which eyes the goblins are gonna be left with."

"Coo-eee, we's got ourselves in a pickle, don't we?" said Edwina, forgetting herself and that she was supposed to always – *always* – act goblin-like.

Dissun and Dudderun laughed. "Ain't no worse'n some of the other stuff we've gotten ourselves into."

Edwina thought it probably was, but chose not to press the issue.

Twelve

*T*he seelie dipped its toes in the pond and looked at the stars' positions. Midnight was nearing and the goblin hadn't yet returned. Disappointment crept into its temperament as it began to think its craving for the milk of a young goat might not be sated. But then it heard a splashing, and it looked up to see not only the many-eyed, red-capped hobgoblin, but also the two boys it'd done a favor for before, and – *pestilence and plague be upon them!* – a dozen unseelies. Seelies aren't so fond of their conniving, smelly cousins. It wasn't so much the conniving, as that was a shared trait. It was the smelliness and unkempt tunics that offended the seelie's senses.

It watched as the assemblage approached, and gritted its teeth when it saw one of the boys leading a swollen-uddered nanny barely older than a kid, the other boy carrying a bucket with a jug inside, and mugs of assorted tiny sizes swinging with their handles looped around the goblin's long fingers.

Drat! thought the seelie. However, while things might not work out quite as the fairy had planned, there was still the favor to be done, and the seelie forced a smile to its pale face.

"Hullo," the seelie waved with faux cheerfulness at the unusual collection of visitors to its mossy stone. It wasn't sure if it had *ever* seen a human, a goblin and an unseelie all in the same place without one trying to eat or otherwise entrap the others.

Since it was Edwina who'd made the deal with the seelie, it was she who spoke first.

"I've brought your goat and milk," she said. "They's still together, but we can sort out how you'd like it delivered." The goblin took a moment to enjoy the disappointed look upon the seelie's face. Then she said, "and we'll be needin' to conclude upon which two eyes it'll be that the goblins'll all be havin' when all's said and done."

"We were starting to wonder if you were ever coming back," the magpie said when Edwina emerged from the grass. The burlap sack hanging from her belt was full and lumpy.

The bird was resting on the rump of the pink pig, and the swine was nibbling at some mushrooms it had just discovered. Edwina wasn't sure if the pig had even noticed she was gone.

"Took a little longer than I'd expected," said the goblin as she strapped the bag filled with clams across the pig's back.

"What's that?" asked the magpie.

"Somethin' for all them multi-eyed goblins to go back as they was before." She removed her cap. "Notice anything diff'rent?"

"Wock!" the magpie squawked. "Your head's back to being just slaggy old skin. No more extra eyeballs!"

"That's right," smiled Edwina. For a tiny, very tiny, moment, she imagined being the hero when she returned with the cure. But only for a fraction's fraction of a moment, because, in truth, goblins have no heroes and she would be repulsed if any goblin were to think of her as one.

"I met the twins," the goblin cackled as they headed home. "They said we're teammates."

The magpie didn't know what to say to this as it had never heard of such a thing: goblin and humans weren't known to be mutually communal.

Edwina looked sideways at the bird. "Don't worry. Them befuddled nitwits can think what they want." She thumped a gnarled thumb towards herself. "I's still a hobgoblin. T'ain'tn't no human ever alive that's gonna collective up with me." She paused and turned, looking back towards the farm. "Although…"

"Although what?" squawked the magpie.

"The way they behave, it don't seem like they know they's gotta curse upon their heads."

"Could be they don't care. I know *I* don't care."

"Or… could be they don't know. Could be that woman never told 'em."

"What of it?" asked the bird.

"Possibly nothing," said Edwina. "Just something good to keep in yer mind. You never know what potentialities might arise."

Back at the pond, Dissun, Dudderun, the seelie and the unseelies, having watched the goblin go, turned back to their own directions home.

"D'ya think she meant it?" Dissun wondered aloud.

"Who?" asked Dudderun.

"That hobgoblin. D'ya think she really thinks we're teammates?"

"Pfftt!" Dudderun snorted. "That old befuddled nitwit can think what she wants. We's still humans. T'ain'tn't no goblin ever alive that's gonna collective up with us." And then he said, "Whoops! What's this?"

It was at that moment that they felt a stickiness wrapped around them and an inability to move came over their bodies.

"Looks like a big fat tongue," said Dissun.

Looking around, they saw it wasn't only themselves that had a tongue wrapped around them and holding them in place. The seelie and unseelies were caught, too.

Each tongue, with one end wrapped around its captive, culminated with its other end inside the mouth of a toad holding a stick-spear like a soldier. Behind the soldier toads sat another, quite large toad. It was three times as big as the other toads, and it was fatter than six of them put together.

Its warts were bigger. Its green was greener. Its yellow eyes were more froggy, and its lipless mouth stretched across from earhole to earhole with a chin beneath that folded over itself like lumpy pudding.

"Wath do you wan uth t' do withum?" said one of the toads. It had difficulty speaking, what with its tongue being used as it was.

"Stop talking," croaked the giant toad. "You sound ridiculous."

The Toad King, for that's what the giant toad was, turned to the hostages. "So it's because of you that my minions were dinner for the goblins."

Dissun and Dudderun, not sure if that had been a statement or a question, chose not to respond just yet.

"It was the goblins' fault," wheedled an unseelie. "We was just helpin' the humans protective themselves."

The toad stared at the unseelie with unblinking frog-eyes.

"And I was just doing them a favor," whined the seelie.

The toad stared at the seelie and blinked its toad-eyes once.

"Do you have anything to say?" the Toad King said to the boys.

"Not as of yet," said Dissun.

"We'd like to take a moment to see what needs sayin, if'n ya don't mind," said Dudderun.

The toads whose tongues were lassoed around the humans and fairies didn't appear very comfortable. But the impression was strongly given that they weren't going to change anything they were doing without the say-so of His Majesty.

"Doesn't matter anyway," said the Toad King. "I'm going to take my revenge upon you regardless of what comes out of your lippy faces."

"What're ya gonna do?" asked Dissun.

"Haven't decided yet," said the Toad King.

The soldier toads looked sideways at each other. Drool was beginning to drip from their widely-open mouths.

"I've never thought about this," said Dudderun. "What does a toad do for revenge?"

"Stuff us full of flies, maybe?" suggested his brother.

"Or might give us a buncha warts."

The boys grew quiet, imagining what their mother might think if they returned home all wart-covered. Dissun shrugged. Dudderun grinned.

"That's just an old wives' tale," croaked the Toad King.

"There it is again," said Dissun. He turned to the Toad King. "By any chance, do you know if it's the wives that're old or if it's the tale?"

The Toad King started to say something, then blinked and stopped.

The tongues of the soldier toads were growing dry and losing their stickiness.

"Well…" the Toad King began, "it's always just been an adage."

"I think it might be the wives that are old," said Dissun, squirming as he spoke, "on accounts of how they's the ones that remembers all them sayin's."

"Naw, them sayin's're older'n grandpa," said Dudderun, wriggling as he spoke, "and that's mighty old."

One of the soldier toads slapped the water with a webbed foot.

The Toad King, deep in wondering, ignored it.

Another soldier toad shifted its feet in the mud.

Still deeply wondering, the Toad King continued to ignore. He stared into the pond water, mulling the question.

"Your highneth," a soldier ventured to speak.

How dare they interrupt my mulling!?! thought the Toad King, and it turned on the soldier who had dared to speak.

The soldier said nothing more, but pointed at Dissun, Dudderun, the seelie and the unseelies who, having wiggled out of the dried tongues that now lay on the ground, were running away.

"Drat!" croaked the Toad King. "After them!"

A best effort was made, but with their dehydrated tongues lolling on the ground and unable to retract back where they belonged, the soldier toads' webbed feet tangled in disarray, and they found it impossible to make chase.

"Thsorry thsir," said one. "But it thseemth we canth go afthter them, whath with our tongueth layin on the dirth ath they areth."

"You're an embarrassment to the Toad Kingdom, you know," croaked the King.

"Yesth thsir," they answered in unison.

"Well, pick up your tongues and we'll sort this out later."

Tongues gathered and rolled back into their wide mouths, the soldier toads hopped in a line behind the Toad King as he made his way to the lily pads.

He climbed onto the largest one. It teetered a little before finding a center point in which to hold the corpulent toad afloat.

The king croaked and licked a fly from the air. He smacked his lips, enjoying the tastiness.

The brain in his toad head mulled about whether it was the wives or the tales that were old.

The Toad King started to deliberate upon whether it might be advantageous to consider a means of exacting revenge upon the deplorable twins, but he fell asleep before coming to any conclusion.

"One for each extra eyeball," Edwina said for the umpteenth time.

Goblins were greedy and had a tendency to gorge themselves on anything within reach with the remotest possibility of edibleness. Hobgoblin arms and legs reached and spread and swung around, with everyone trying to be the first in line. A great deal of cursing and insults intertwined among the appendages.

Edwina was tempted to simply dump the bag of clams on the ground and let the rabble go for a what-have-you. But she'd resisted that temptation. Each clam was charmed to remove a toad-eye from the goblin that ate it. If they ate too many, the clams would start taking what else they could, be it eyeballs, toes, navels or anything else handy. As much as Edwina thought that might be a treat to see, she knew the goblin-wrath that would ensue would prove that enjoyable treat fleeting and with little residue. So she stood her ground, dipping her arm into the sack, retrieving one clam at a time, and handing them out on an as-needed basis.

Soon, a cacophony of sucking and popping sounds fluttered amidst the goblins as they gulped down the clams whole, shell and all; and the clams sucked the toad-eyes from the outsides of the goblinned bodies to the insides of their shelled mouths. Engorged on toad-eyes, the clams swelled in the stomachs of the goblins, bloating their bellies to an unnatural extension. The goblins looked at one another, at first pointing and cackling at the other's expansion, then, upon realizing they were in the same predicament, bellowing snarled curses the likes of which had never been heard of before because they'd only just been invented.

What followed was a second cacophony. This one, however, was of the sounds of retching and heaving and groaning and gasping for air. The vomited clams, each still being in one piece because goblins never chew their food, hopped away towards the stream that would lead to the pond.

The burlap sack empty, Edwina nodded in self-satisfaction, and retrieved another, smaller bag from her belt She looked inside and counted the clams. Reassured that she had reserved enough, she climbed aboard her pink pig and headed in the direction of the many-eyed likho.

Clicking sounds startled the Toad King from his sleep. Snapping and clacking, like little castanets, all around him.

"Who's there?" the king croaked.

He was answered by more clicking, snapping and clacking.

Peering into the murkiness, his eyes slowly grew accustomed to the dark and he saw what it was.

"Soldiers!" he grunted, nearly falling off his lily-pad.

"Sire!" one of them called back.

"Get over here!" commanded the warted, green monarch.

"We can't, sire. Sorry."

"Why not!?"

"The clams, sire."

The Toad King looked around at the clams floating around his lily-pad and everywhere across the pond. Wide open, with blinking toad-eyes that stared up at him as they bobbed on the water's surface.

Well, thought the king, *I guess at least I'm surrounded by my minions again.* He grinned, as only a fat toad with no lips can grin, and allowed himself to fall back asleep.

Thirteen

I n a wide and open field, given ample berth by the woods surrounding it, stood a lone tree. Its bark was black as if charred by an ancient fire, although it had never felt a flame, and the top was ragged with age. Bare branches stretched up and out, waning to long and spindly sticks. Where it touched the ground, the trunk bisected with thick roots burrowing into the soil, sending fibrous tentacles in every direction. The tree was lone, alone and, vaguely, lonely. And it was hungry. And, also, just now, it was becoming very irritated.

The vague loneliness was due to the nature of the likho in that, except for the rare occasion when one might be invited over for stew, being alone tended to be their choice. In fact, this likho was reveling in it.

The hunger was for the same reason as anyone might be hungry.

The reason for the irritation was the sight of a goblin with a spotted head and flappy skin, riding her pink pig across the field in the tree's direction. A magpie was perched on the pig's round rump. The likho opened one eye, then shut it tight. It shuddered and thought, *Floating like an old driftwood in a putrid bog would be preferable to this.*

The likho held as still as it could. Perhaps, with a bit of luck, Edwina would think it was just an old tree and continue on to wherever it was she was going. But there was no such luck to be had.

"I knows it's you," the goblin called out. She stood at the base of the tree, near but not too close to its rooted feet.

"Sshhh!" hissed the likho. "I'm hunting."

Edwina held up a rough burlap sack. "I broughts ya some rabbits."

Dropping its branching arms, the likho sighed, pulled its feet from the ground and sat next to the hobgoblin. It peered into the sack.

"No charms or fairy witchery?" the likho hesitated.

"Naw," answered the goblin. "That was a whole other thing." She had thought of asking about the meaning of the curse, but had decided not to bring the subject up on the chance that, if it *wasn't* against the bag of eyes, it could always be adjusted to include such things. *We can address that at another time*, Edwina thought.

"This is very nice of you, Edwina," the likho said as it opened the sack and let the rabbits drop into its mouth and down its gullet. "What do you want?"

"Now," Edwina wheedled, "can't a friend bring another friend some lunch just to be nice?"

"You're a hobgoblin," the likho smacked its bark-lips. "You're not nice, and you don't have any friends." It got up to leave. "You and I are especially not-friends."

Edwina scrambled to hop onto one of the likho's enormous feet as it walked away. "Well, that just hurts," she said, grappling the root with her boney legs and arms.

"It's because of you that I have the eyes of a frog." The likho shook its leg, trying to dislodge the clinging Edwina, but she'd attached herself with the claw-like nails of her fingers and toes.

"If it wasn't for me, you'd have no eyes at all." The little, yet very strong, goblin held tight to the root-foot. Her skin flapped and her bulbous rump jiggled with every step the tree took.

While the likho would never admit it, the hobgoblin was right. It wasn't her fault it'd ripped its own eyes out, even if she *did* collect them and give them to her daughter. However, it felt much better to blame someone else than to admit the truth.

"Okay! Okay!" Edwina shouted upwards. "I *do* want something."

The likho stopped walking and looked down at its foot. "And what is that?"

"I'm a'goin' away." Edwina climbed off the tree's foot and stepped back so she could see its face as she spoke.

"Away?" the likho raised a knotted eyebrow.

"Far away."

"How far?"

"Far enough that I don'ts gotsta hear no more complainin' from them toad-eyed hags and their tradition-bogged husbands."

"You're going to need to go very, *very* far to do that. So, what is it that you want?"

"I was wonderin' if you'd want to come with me."

Shaking its head but saying no words, the likho began to walk again.

Edwina chased after it. The pink pig desperately chased after them both. The magpie, being afforded wings, flew to the tree and hooked its feet onto a branch.

"I should've just eaten you raw," grumbled the likho, lengthening its stride.

"Raw goblin ain't no good for you," Edwina claimed, not really knowing whether that was true. "You'd've just gotten indigestion. And, besides," she panted, "that woman would still've used her chalk."

"Not if you and your husband had eaten her baby first."

"You caughts us up for yer stew," protested the out-of-breath hobgoblin. "We never got the chance."

Edwina's face splatted into the back of a barked-hind-leg when the likho stopped. The pig tumbled into the goblin's backside and bounced backwards several feet. When it stopped rolling, it trotted closer to the likho and began munching on some grass stuck between the tree's toes.

"And now, I hear, you're *friends*," the likho sneered.

"Hah! That's what *they* think!"

"It's what everybody thinks. You had the chance to feed them to the meanest thing you could find – and there were lots of volunteers for that job – but you skipped away with a bag of clams."

112

"I done what I had to do to get everyone's eyes back to normal," Edwina argued, almost sincerely. "As normal as could be, that is. Wasn't nothin' could be done about them all bein' the eyes of toads."

The rabbits were working their way through the likho's insides, searching for a knothole. *Perhaps I should have chewed before swallowing*, the tree thought.

Fourteen

"*H*ow far d'ya think we'll hafta go?" Dissun kicked a rock down the dirt path.

"No way of knowin'," said Dudderun, "but if'n we don't find none, we just keep on walkin' and seek our fortunes."

Dissun nodded in agreement, and the two boys continued their march.

Earlier that morning, their mother had introduced them to a squealing, red faced thing and told them it was their new baby sister.

Shortly after the introduction, Dissun and Dudderun had packed some lunches and headed down the road in search of the nearest witch. Or their fortunes. They hadn't decided yet which they wanted to find first, but were certain they didn't want it to include a baby sister.

"You know fer sure we're gonna be babysittin' all the time. And I'll bet there's no amount of old goat milk that'll get the Unseelies to do it for us."

"Sure would be nice if the witch could make it into a little brother," Dissun said with some wistfulness. "Leastwise, if she can't get rid of the thing all together, that is."

They walked a bit more, thinking about the horrors of a baby sister, the unknowns of what fortunes might be down the road, and whether whichever witch they found might just eat them for dinner instead.

The pig was quite content being rocked in the crook of the tree's elbow, and it dozed with a happy smile beneath its snout.

Edwina was comfortable, and had been enjoying herself, complaining and grousing for the better part of the journey.

The rabbits, having found a loose knothole, were thankful to be freed from the belly of the tree.

The likho, however, was neither content, nor comfortable. It did, however, feel a bit relieved to have the rabbits no longer running up and down its innards. Although, as far as the likho was concerned, the extra kick they gave as they exited was rude and entirely unnecessary.

"I need to take a break," the likho announced. The rabbits may have departed, but they'd left behind gifts that the tree needed to shake out.

The likho gently set the pig down, and it began snuffling for mushrooms.

Edwina, was unceremoniously dropped to the ground , and she tumbled over herself, getting her ears tangled in the hairs from her armpits. When she gained her ground and a bit of composure, the hobgoblin found a lumpy spot in the grass that looked comfortable for her odd-shaped rear-end. She sat, found a stick with which to pick her teeth, and waited for the likho to clear itself of what the rabbits had left behind.

The magpie flitted down from its branch, stood on the goblin's shoulder, and proceeded to have some lunch, picking bugs from between the creases in the goblin's hide. It was swallowing down a rather large beetle when it looked to one side and saw a flying broom laden with howling cats and a round, dandelion-headed woman. The spectacle was encased in a cloud of cat hair.

Edwina watched as the vision flew overhead, tracking where it was going and determining where it might stop. When the likho finished hopping and shaking, she jumped on a low branch. "Let's go!" she shouted, just a little too enthusiastically.

Suspicious, the tree looked down at the goblin. "What's the rush?"

"Oh… no rush at all. Take yer time." Edwina scrambled up the trunk to an upper branch, and looked across the hills in the direction the broom had flown.

The likho sat down, crossing its enormous wooden legs. The roots that were its toes dangled lazily.

Edwina squirmed, but held her tongue as long as she could. Which wasn't very long. "Does ya have to take yer restin' right now?"

"I'm taking your advice," the tree leaned back and rested its entire body across the ground, resembling a felled log.

Her upper perch now being at ground level, Edwina scooted off the branch. "Takin' yer time ain't the same as stoppin' all together."

"You said you wanted to get as far away as possible," said the tree. "We're fairly far away. Perhaps not as far as possible, but…" it closed its frog eyes for a nap.

"We's gotsta get goin!" Edwina skittered around the tree, attempting, without success, to lift it off the ground.

The magpie, still holding onto the folds of the goblin skin, pulled a small bug from the goblin's ear and gulped it down. "She wants to follow the Moggyfrau," it squawked.

"Blast you, you no good corvid!" Edwina swatted at the bird.

"The Moggyfrau?" The likho raised itself to its elbowed branches and leered at the hobgoblin. "Well, *that's* interesting."

Edwina spat at the magpie, then turned to the tree, and, with a grotesquely saccharine smile, said, "It's just for a quick visit."

"*You* want to visit the *Moggyfrau?*"

"D'ya see that?" Dissun watched the puff of cat-hair flying across the sky.

"I don't think I've never seen nothin' like it," said Dudderun, shading his eyes with the palm of his hand. "Looked like there was a broom inside'a all've that, with a buncha cats ridin' on it."

"And a little round lady," said Dissun. "You think that could be one of them witches we's lookin' for?"

"If'n our mum would let us bet on anything, I'd lay a wager on that possibility."

"Maybe she can help us out," Dissun said.

"She's sure to be powerful enough, what with all them cats."

It was a well-known fact that the more cats a witch has, the more powerful their magic is.

"I'm figurin' she's probably got a gob more felines at her house," Dudderun added.

"Then we ought to be followin' her," said Dissun. "Don'tcha think?"

Dudderun nodded, and the brothers turned to walk in the direction in which the cat-lady had flown.

Swooping on her broom around the chimney first, just for a bit of fun, the Moggyfrau expertly landed on the thatched roof. She waited for the thirteen cats to jump off before disembarking herself, then she held up the broom by its knotted and gnarled shaft, and tossed it in the air. It rose and twirled in a happy dance, then fluttered down to the porch, floated through an open window, and rested itself on the floor in front of the fireplace. Several cats climbed on top of it and promptly fell asleep.

The witch, a round little woman with matching girth and height, stood on the roof, the toes of her bare feet grabbing at the straw. If two cats stood one atop the other, she might have been able to see over the top of them. Stout arms and legs stuck out from her black tunic and trousers, which were covered with cat hair. The gray hair on her small dandelion of a head appeared never to have been introduced to a brush or comb. Her plump body balanced with an unexpected agility as she stepped around the multitude of cats across the rooftop. Just as she approached the chimney, her eye caught something in the distance. One of the larger cats, having opened its lethargic eyes just at that moment, saw it, too.

The Moggyfrau watched the strange sight making its way over the hill a short distance away. "What in the darnednation…?"

"I don't think I've ever seen anything like that," said the cat. He was black with short, sleek hair, whiskers that twitched and a long tail with a tip that flicked back and forth.

"Can't say as I have either," the woman said. "But I know who it is. And I've got some what-for I'll be wantin' to give 'er.'"

The cat jumped gracefully from the roof. Seventeen more cats also jumped off. The rest remained, sleeping and bathing themselves in the sun.

The Moggyfrau clambered down the side of the chimney, cat hair wafting off her clothes with each step, and headed for the door, hopping over and around the carpet of cats lazing across the porch.

"Who is it?" asked the black cat, following her.

"That hobgoblin, wassername – Edwina." The cats sleeping against the door slid across the wood-slatted floor when she pushed it open and tromped inside.

"Have you seen what's coming our way?" asked the calico, laying atop the clean dishes and looking out the window.

"Yes, we have," said the woman.

"A tree….," the calico squinted and peered, "carrying a pink pig. And, I'm not sure, but it looks like a hobgoblin riding on one of its branches."

"That tree's a likho. Mind yourselves around it as them things're carnivorous," said the woman. "And that goblin's

Edwina," she said, grabbing the broom, displacing the cats who'd just begun napping on top of it

"I'll be back," announced the old woman as she stormed out to the porch, clutching the broom with both of her small, stout hands. She straddled the broom, and thirteen cats jumped onboard just before she soared into the air, mewling and caterwauling as they went.

Fifteen

*E*dwina was having second thoughts.

"Aiyeeee…" she howled. "Never mind! We don't gotsta go this way. Over yonder across them other hills is just as fine."

The likho smirked as it watched the flying poof of cat hair coming towards them. "But I thought you wanted to see the Moggyfrau."

"I've changed me mind."

"Well, I'm not changing direction now. Not when it's just getting interesting."

The pig squealed, unsure if it should be frightened by the goblin's protestations or happy that, having stopped, it was sure to soon find itself on the ground where it could snuffle for some more mushrooms.

"Woot! Woot!" the magpie squawked, hopping up and down on the pig's head.

"Shut up, ya stupid bird!" Edwina barked. She peeled herself from the grips of the branches and fell to the ground, then jumped up and started running. She didn't know where to run to, just that she needed to run away from where she was at the moment.

The likho, after setting the pig down, reached out a branch, grabbed the goblin, and held her aloft with her feet paddling in the air. The tree lazily swung the goblin back and forth.

"Let me go!" Edwina squealed. "There's cats comin' our way, and'a overripe old witch lady to boot."

"I can see that," said the likho. "And, judging by what's reaching our ears, those cats are very much alive, aren't they?"

"Confound it! You know goblins don't like cats unless'n they're good and dead." Edwina bit at the tree branch holding her, getting her teeth stuck in the bark. "Ith baf lufk t'buh arounth 'emf," she said, then, yanking her teeth out of the wood, repeated herself. "It's bad luck t'be around 'em."

"Unless they're dead."

"Well, them's alive that're comin' with that witch. Let me go!"

"Too late," said the likho when the Moggyfrau landed in front of them.

"Aiyeeee, and nooo-nooo-nooo…" howled the hobgoblin, working up to a crescendo, struggling against the likho's grip.

At the likho's feet, the cats joined in with the goblin, caterwauling and yowling, with hissing in between.

The magpie studied them, then flitted to an upper branch.

"Knock that off!" the Moggyfrau yelled at Edwina. She turned to her cats. "Cooo…. cooo…. there ya go…. them's a pretties…."

"Hello, Moggyfrau," the Likho said.

"Hello, likho," the old lady responded, grabbing the broomstick. Taking a step closer, she squinted at the tree. "Is them frog-eyes you got there?"

The likho sighed. "Yes…"

The Moggyfrau looked at the suspended goblin. "Would I be correct in guessing *she* had somethin' to do with that?"

"You would be," said the likho.

"Trouble, that's all them goblins are," said the Moggyfrau. "Exceptin' your type, that is," she added, nodding towards the likho.

"You're not wrong there, either. But this one," it shook the branch holding the hobgoblin, rattling Edwina's teeth and making the folds of her skin flap like tongues lapping water, "she's an acquaintance of mine and it's a preponderance upon me to do what I can to keep her unharmed, to an extent."

Edwina grinned. "I *told* ya we was friends," she called down.

The likho harrumphed and gave the goblin an extra shake, then asked the Moggyfrau, "Is there any particular reason you might be focused upon this one?"

The Moggyfrau raised the broom and jabbed the stick in Edwina's direction. "Let's ask her about that bag of cat tails she gave that empty-headed daughter of hers."

"Cat tails?" the likho directed this question towards the goblin.

"I hads to get that bag of eyes back!" Edwina snorted. "Mildred, lovely kin though she may be, don't know how to take care o'things. So's I took 'em back."

"Well," considered the likho, "that explains you wanting to get as far away as possible. But I find it hard to believe she let you just *take* them."

"She traded for 'em," sniffed Edwina.

"Tell 'em what you used in your tradin'," snarled the Moggyfrau.

"I don't think I want to know – " the likho started.

"Cat tails!" shrieked the Moggyfrau. A chorus of howling cats joined in.

"What kind of cat tails?" the likho asked.

"Not the kind that grows by the pond, I can tell you that!" the old woman screeched, wailing cats harmoniously hissing along.

"They weren't using 'em no more," Edwina yelled defiantly. "Them cats was already dead. I found 'em that way. So's I gived Mildred the tails." She left out the fact that a good stew had resulted from the remainder of the dead felines.

"Dead?" asked the likho.

"Dead and buried," answered Edwina.

"That's right. And you diggin' 'em up ain't neither proper nor respectful," the Moggyfrau pointed a plump finger at Edwina. "Maybe we should see about teaching you somethin' about reverence." She made a sweeping gesture from the cats to the goblin dangling in the tree. "Get her!"

Without an iota of hesitation, the thirteen cats jumped into action. Snarling, mewling and hissing, they ran up the likho's trunk, digging their claws in as they climbed towards the branch holding their quarry. The tree looked like it was dancing a jig, shaking its bark, grabbing at the cats and flicking and throwing them to the ground.

The pig with peculiar amusement, and the magpie, who'd decided on top of the swine was a much safer place to be at the moment, watched with delight.

"Hah! I'm'a gonna get you, you fetid aberration of all that's nature," the Moggyfrau sneered, hooking a stubby leg over the broomstick and squatting for extra spring in her liftoff.

Enough is enough! decided the likho,. Twigs curled around every cat, and a strong branch caught up the Moggyfrau and held her extended opposite the hobgoblin. The broom fell to the ground.

It suddenly became very quiet.

"You two…" the likho wasn't sure which words should be next, but there were several it wished to say and most of them weren't polite.

"She started it!" squealed the goblin. "Comin' after us like she did."

"What's that?" countered the witch. "You dug up my precious cats and gave their tails to that daft daughter of yours."

"They wasn't usin' 'em no more."

"And what'd you do with the rest of the poor, dead kitties? Hmmm?"

"Stop it!" The likho shook the two squabblers. "I'm done with the both of you!"

It pulled a sizeable chunk of bark from its trunk and swaddled the annoying pair within it, plus all thirteen cats. A long vine slithered around and around the disgruntled parcel, tying itself into a nice bow on top.

"Ack! Not with them accursed cats!" screeched Edwina, wrestling against the encasing.

"Don't you dare snug me in with that wretched, stinkin' wotsnaught!" commanded the Moggyfrau with no effect.

The baker's dozen of cats spluttered, hissed and spat with indignation at the turn of events, then grew eerily silent, keening their eyes on the goblin with every bit of aloof acrimony they could muster.

The likho threw the bickering bundle across the fire and chucked the broom after them.

"I'm going home," said the tree, turning to the pig and the magpie. "You can follow them, stay here, or come with me."

The pink pig and the black bird looked at each other. The pig oinked at the tree goblin.

"No, I won't eat you," said the likho.

With a happy squeal, the pig trotted over and hopped into a cupped branch that lifted the swine up and tucked it securely in to the elbow of a thick bough.

The magpie flew to the craggy top of the tree. It watched the ball of witch and goblin and cat until it was a speck then disappeared. The bird shrugged, and made itself comfortable for the ride home.

Sixteen

*T*he boys watched the howling bundle fly towards them, then land with several bounces and come to a stop a short distance from where they stood.

After considering their options and letting curiosity win the joust, they belly-crawled at first, then walked upright when it appeared whatever it was inside the neatly wrapped bundle wasn't making its way free any time soon. They stood, looking at the thing, Dudderun chewing thoughtfully on a twig and Dissun nibbling meditatively on a sprig of grass.

Dudderun removed the twig from between his teeth and used it to point at the swaddling of bark. "I think I recognize that bark from when we was bein' carried by that likho to its cave."

Dissun rolled the sprig from one side of his mouth to the other. "And I'm pretty sure we're familiar with one of them voices coming from inside." Holding the grass between his thumb and forefinger, he called out, "Is that you, the hobgoblin Edwina, inside'a there?"

The fitful arguing of the goblin and Moggyfrau, and the snarling of the cats came to an abrupt stop. Whispering could be heard, then a voice dripped, "Yes…?" There was some hissing, and Edwina added, "And who might I be havin' the pleasure of speakin' to?"

"Aww, you knows us," said Dudderun, matching the drippyness.

"Oooo… ! My teammates!"

Dissun and Dudderun exchanged glances. Dissun grinned a smile even his mother wasn't fond of. Dudderun grinned back.

"Judgin' by all the cat hair that's a-waftin' around, would it be safe to say the other one in there's the cat lady?" asked Dudderun.

"I prefer to be called *Moggyfrau* if it's all the same to you." said a voice the boys didn't recognize. "Who're you?"

"Them's my teammates," cackled Edwina.

"Yeah, but I still don't know who they are."

"I'm Dis— " Dissun started to say, thumbing his chest.

"Watchit," warned Dudderun, jabbing his elbow at his brother's ribs. "Mum says to never give a goblin yer name."

"You're the humans that took space upaways by the pond?" said the Moggyfrau.

"A couple of 'em, at least," said Dudderun. "Who're you?"

At that point, the broom caught up with them, jamming itself into the ground and standing upright with its whisk at attention.

The boys knew a witch's broom when they saw one.

"And you's a witch, right?" asked Dissun.

Dissun turned to Dudderun, "I hear cats inside'a there. Lotsa cats."

"She must be one've the most powerful witches around," said Dissun.

"Oh, I am," called out the Moggyfrau. "Mighty powerful." She paused, then added, "Is there any chance you might be lettin' me out of this confinement?"

"Don't let her out! She'll eats the two of you," squawked Edwina. "Let me out instead."

"Witches don't eat children," said the Moggyfrau, "that's just an old wive's tale."

"There's that old wive's tales thing again," said Dissun. "Maybe you know. Is it the wives or the tale that's old?"

"Confound it, you little urchins, let me outta here!" Edwina snapped, kicking at the encasement of bark. Cats mewled and hissed, and the goblin whined, "You gotsta get me aways from these wretched felines."

"We can't very well let the one of you out without letting the other out as well," said Dudderun. "And, regardless of your assurances, we ain't too sure we won't get eaten once you're out."

"Teammate or not, you goblins've got a fairly nasty reputation," said Dissun.

"That's the kindest thing anyone's said to me for a long time," said Edwina, sounding sincere. "I promis's, hobgoblin's honor. I won't eats you."

"I promise the same," said the Moggyfrau, adding in a grumble under her breath, "not that I need to, seein' as how I wouldn't've done so anyhow."

Dissun gingerly stepped forward and pulled at the end of the vine, untying the bow. Both boys jumped back, just in case either of the two captives changed their mind.

The bark sprung open, and the Moggyfrau bounced out, her round body rolling across the grass and coming to a stop against her upright broom. Edwina popped in the opposite direction, tumbling feet over ears, and finishing with her arms and legs sticking straight in the air. The thirteen cats jumped out, looked around, ruffled the skin under their coats, and sat down and proceeded to bathe themselves. After all, being cats, this was exactly as they had intended for everything to be.

"You think we should ask her?" Dudderun muttered sideways to his brother.

"I don't see as to why not," Dissun muttered back.

"Ask who?" said Edwina, arms and legs still pointing upwards, thinking that remaining in such a position might not be all that bad.

"Not you," both boys answered.

Edwina snorted, but otherwise held her tongue.

"Well," said the Moggyfrau, "you *did* help me out of that situation. I suppose I can hear you out."

"Well…" Dissun shuffled his feet and scratched the back of his grubby neck. He'd never talked to a witch before and wasn't sure of the etiquette.

Dudderun, also unsure of the etiquette, finished his brother's thought. "We've got this new baby sister, you see…"

Edwina sat up. "A baby, you say?"

Ignoring the goblin, the Moggyfrau asked, "And what of it?"

The boys looked at each other. Taking a deep breath, Dissun said, "Is there any chance you can send it back where's it came from?"

"What's that?" asked the Moggyfrau.

"We don't want nothin' bad to happen to it, we assure you," Dudderun said to the witch. "We just don't wants to be doin' no babysittin' is all. So, if'n you don't mind, we'd surely appreciate it if you could sees that it goes back to wherever our mum got it from."

The Moggyfrau squinted, looking from one boy to the other, judging whether they were joking and coming to the conclusion that they were not.

"I don't think anyone can do that," she said.

"I can take care of it," Edwina called to them. "If that witch ain't strong enough to do it, I surely can."

"It's not a matter of power. And we know what *you'll* do with it." The Moggyfrau scowled at the goblin.

"Awww… I'll give it a good home," wheedled the hobgoblin, unable to stop the drool from dripping off her fleshy lower lip.

"We knows what you'll do. You's gonna *eats* her!" said Dissun. "Our mum told us all about you and how you thought *we'd* be a nice little dinner."

"But we're teammates now," protested Edwina, holding her arms out to either side.

The boys glowered at Edwina for a good bit of time, ensuring she knew they weren't falling for any promises she might make pertaining to their baby sister. Then they turned back to the witch.

"Well, if ya can't send her back," said Dudderun, "maybe you can make her a bit more enjoyable."

"And what would you propose that might be?"

"If we gotsta keep the thing, at least if it was a baby brother it might be preferable," said Dissun.

"You just want it to be more fun for you, is that right?"

The boys nodded vigorously, feeling they were getting somewhere.

"All right then," the Moggyfrau grinned.

If the boys had had more experience with witches, they might have recognized the grin. It was a mischievous one, not much different from their own.

The Moggyfrau ran her dimpled hands across her tunic, gathering a handful of cat hairs. "Here," she said, holding it out to the boys, "sprinkle this over the baby, and I guarantee you'll be having times you hadn't thought possible."

Seventeen

*T*he sun was rising over the far mountains, shooting out colors of orange and pink, poking its beams through the clouds, and sending ablutions across the world. Edwina could have been watching it, but she wasn't.

The pond was gurgling with frog-eyed clams, and the King Toad sat on his lily-pad happily snapping flies from the air just before the jumping fish could get to the tasty morsels. Edwina could have been watching this, too, but she wasn't.

Scythed crops lay across the fields, waiting to be gathered, and cows and sheep and pigs were blinking in the morning light as they emerged from the barn. Behind them, twelve short and thin fairies with long, green hair, prodded the livestock with long sticks. Edwina could have been watching this, and that was what she was doing.

Perched in a tree – which wasn't easy with skinny legs and arms, a bulbous and rippled belly, and ears that kept getting in the way as she climbed – the goblin slitted her eyes to a tight squint, and watched the farm wake up.

"Leave me behind, will they…" she grumbled.

On the previous day, she'd been abandoned by the likho, who'd whacked her across the distance then walked away carrying her pig and the magpie; and the Moggyfrau, who'd jumped on her broom and flown away with her horde of wretched felines; and the horrid twins, who'd stuffed their pockets full of cat hair and gone home to where there was a newly-born and probably very tasty sibling awaiting. Edwina couldn't very well perform a comeuppance upon the likho or Moggyfrau, but she found it easy to lay the bounty of the blame for her desertion on the boys and, therefore, assign the full brunt of comeuppance upon them. (Not to mention, the potential of such comeuppance being followed with a tasty infant wasn't something the hobgoblin was willing to pass up.) The branches below Edwina were soaking wet from her drooling at the very thought.

A bolt of howling shrieks jolted her from the reverie, and Edwina nearly bit her lolling tongue. They were the shrieks that only a mother who's looked into the patience-barrel and found it absolutely empty can make, followed by crashing sounds and curses that impressed the hobgoblin with their inventiveness.

"What's this?" Edwina grinned, watching the woman storm from the house to the barn, picking up sticks along the way, one after the other, each larger and more ergonomically club-like than the one before. Under one arm, she held a bundle.

Edwina sniffed the air. Yes. Inside that bundle was a baby. She sniffed a few more times. A newborn, fresh and tasty. "Ouch!" she yelped when the knob of her boney knee dug into her fleshy tongue that was dangling from her mouth and across the branch. She rolled the tongue back behind her jagged teeth and wiped the spittle from her chin, then returned her attention to the commotion taking place among the humans.

The woman went into the barn. Chickens flew out. More crashing. A great deal more cursing. The barn door opened, with the woman holding it wide, and the twin boys hastily trotted out carrying the bundle between them.

"Hmmm...." said the goblin, and she climbed down from the tree and hid in the grass where she could follow them at a convenient distance.

"How d'ya think mum knew it was us?" asked Dudderun.

"Process of elimination, I suppose," said Dissun, "on a list that's shortened to only us two."

The boys walked along the path, trading the bundle between them every so often.

"Who'd've known a baby could be so heavy?" said Dissun.

"Well, at least she ain't squealin' none," said Dudderun. "but she sure is startin' to reek up an aroma."

The Frog King watched as they passed the pond, his eyes keen on keeping them at a distance from him and his minions. Toad soldiers flanked him on either side, pointing their spear-sticks at the boys. Clams, each filled with the single eye of a frog, clicked open and shut in a strange kind of blinking as they floated on the water's surface and watched the twins go by.

"He's still mad at us, I guess," said Dissun, nodding at the toads. "I don't suppose he can be blamed for that."

"Aw," said Dudderun, "he'll get over it – " He stopped midsentence when the sound of a clanking bell came to his ears. Looking back, he said, "What's this?"

"Hold up… a minute… will ya?" the unseelie had trouble getting the words out due to the uneven bouncing atop the rod-straight and boney back of the oldest goat from the herd. Eleven more unseelies bounced behind the first.

"What're *you* doing here?" asked Dissun when the goat-riding unseelies reached them.

"We're comin' with you."

"What about the chores?" said Dudderun. "You're s'posed to be keepin' 'em done in exchange for sleepin' in the loft. That was the deal."

"We was thinking," one of the unseelies towards the back of the row said, "won't your mother get suspicious when she sees chores bein' done whilst she knows you two are away?"

Dissun looked at Dudderun. "They've got a point," he said.

"And we brought our own food," said an unseelie from the middle of the row. It patted an oversized hand on the old goat's hide.

"You all get weird when you drink this old nannie's milk," said Dudderun.

"We promise we'll wait until bedtime," said the first unseelie.

The boys nodded, then Dudderun had an idea. "How's about if we strap this here baby sister across the goat?"

"Good idea," said Dissun, "my arms can't carry the thing much more."

"Plus the goat's own pungents might be hopefully overpower her stinkiness." Everyone's eyes widened and heads nodded at this potential benefit.

Using tangled strands of their long green hair, the unseelies tied the bundle to the boney rump of the goat with the hopes that the emissions coming from the rear end of the animal might overpower those emitting from the baby. Then they turned their twelve noses as far forward as they could, and the odd company of travelers continued down the path.

"You ever seen a Moggyfrau?" asked Dissun.

"Not up-close," answered the unseelie riding in the front of the row. "She don't like fairies too much."

"She well enough likes the seelies," said one of the unseelies down the row.

"That ain't the same thing," said the first unseelie. "Them seelies ain't normal, what with their glowin' and floatin' hair."

The eleven unseelies behind the first muttered in agreement.

"Well," said Dudderun, "we've got to find her somehow. Gotta make things right."

Dissun snorted. "I wouldn't call it *right*. More like back to how it was before we sprinkled it with magic cat hairs. Ain't *nothin'* right about this here baby just showin' up outta nowhere like it did."

The unseelies looked at the boys, then at each other, and shrugged their skinny shoulders.

"We know where she lives," said one of the unseelies. "The Moggyfrau, that is."

"I thought you didn't like bein' up-close," said Dissun.

"One way to keep from bein' up-close is to know where she's gonna be," answered the unseelie.

"Knowin' where we're goin' *would* be mighty helpful," said Dudderun. "S'better'n wandering all over the place just hopin' to run across her."

Everyone nodded, even the goat, and they continued their trodding down the dirt path.

Not far behind, the hobgoblin slunk through the grass, her nose palpitating with the scent of baby wafting behind the ensemble. Aroma of infant… plus… something else familiar, but…

"Umphck!" Edwina nearly choked when yet another infant-associated fragrance floated into her nostrils. "Gechk!" she gagged when the tang of goat joined in. As much as goblins appreciated a good and fetid bouquet, these were smells that were too much even for her. Shoving two crooked fingers into the holes of her nose in an attempt to block the smell, she stood so she could see over the grass. Eyes watering from the olfactory attack, the goblin opted to use her sense of sight for the time being even if it meant tracking through thick, goblin tears.

Eighteen

"**M**aybe we should dunk her in a bucket," Dissun suggested.

"Yeah, but we don't got one of those," said Dudderun. He and his brother had run from the barn so quickly, they barely had time to pick up the lunch their mother had thrown at them when she chased them out.

"Well, we gotsta clean her up somehow," said Dissun.

In front of them lay their baby sister, with her twitching whiskers and pointed ears. Her cat-eyed gaze made the boys feel unsettled.

"I'm not sure I like how she's a'lookin' at us," said Dudderun.

"Yeah, it's like she's just – watchin' – and it's kinda creepin' me out."

But the gaze wasn't at the forefront of their worries at this particular moment. What *was* of concern was that everything she had eaten and digested for the past day was now pasted and soaked into her bunting. The only thing worse than the smell was the thought that, somehow, it needed to be cleaned up.

"There's a stream not too far away," said Dudderun, "maybe we can dip her into that."

"Oh, no you don't!" said an unseelie. "We takes our baths in that stream."

The twelve unseelies and the two boys sat, looking at the smelly infant, considering their options.

"Maybe…," said Dissun.

"What?" said Dudderun.

"You think, maybe, if we just left her for a while, like, didn't do nothin' and just let her be, you think maybe, I dunno, everything might dry up?"

Dudderun thought for a moment. "If everything's dried out maybe we could just flake it all off with a stick or somethin'."

"That was kinda my thought. Sorta like we do when we're all muddy from feedin' the hogs."

The unseelies exchanged glances, but kept their thoughts to themselves because suggesting any other options might incur the necessity for them to provide an example, and that was something none of them was anxious to do.

Feeling things were settled, Dissun and Dudderun decided, since there was nothing much more to do, it was a good time for a nap and they rolled over and went to sleep.

Moving upwind from the odor, the unseelies, having been sneaking sips of the old goat's milk from jugs hidden beneath their tunics and finding themselves in a lethargic lull, found a spot to pile atop one another and were soon snoozing with contented belches.

The goat wagged its short tail and burped up an afternoon snack of cud. Being the only one in the group that didn't mind the stench wafting from the baby, it lay down next to the purring infant, closed its slotted eyes, and dozed.

From a close-enough distance, Edwina made a poultice of grass and leaves, and shoved as much as she could up into her nostrils. Even by goblin standards, the infant was emanating a profuse and painful aroma, and Edwina needed a barrier against even the slightest trickle. When she heard the symphony of snoring, she slithered up to the baby, snatched it, and belly-crawled away into the underbrush.

"Roasted, boiled or raw…" Edwina considered her options. "Pickled is tasty, but takes too long. But maybe if I save a few pieces…" She sat next to the shallow hole she'd dug and filled with water, and in which she'd set the baby to wash itself.

At least it's not making a buncha noise, Edwina thought.

Then she thought, *Why isn't it making a buncha noise?*

And then, after standing up to take a better look, the goblin thought, *Where did it go?*

Wunmor, which was the baby's name, was having fun. She'd got the name in much the same way her brothers had gotten theirs. Meaning, the taxman had asked her grandpa and he'd pointed into the crib and said "Heh, dere's one more."

Up until yesterday, Wunmor's life had been a fairly dull sequence of eating, sleeping, and watching whatever floated within view above her crib – faces of a woman, an old man, and what looked like a giant squirrel. But then, last night, her brothers had come home and sprinkled cat hairs all over her and ever since then everything was better. Her round tummy, smooth as the day she was born, now blended into a lovely blend of orange and red fur that went down to what were now the hindlegs of a cat. The fur was the same color as the hair her mother had tied in a knot at the top of her head. Her arms and little hands were still those of a human baby, but her fingers had grown nails that could grow curiously long and then retract when she thought for them to. She could see in the dark with her feline pupils, the hearing in her fur-covered pointed ears was acute, and the sense of smell with her pink triangle of a nose was delightful. Whiskers tickled her face, and, once the swaddling was removed, it could be seen that a tail had grown behind her. To cheerily top things off, her day had been spent watching the world from the rump of a goat.

Her mother had, unfortunately, swaddled her into a tight bundle, and her alimentary canal couldn't be stopped. But now, having been freed of the bindings, and after tolerating a bit of water, she was fresh and ready for a good meal.

Something scurried past Wunmor's feet, and she pounced into the tall grass after it. The baby was licking bits from between her fingers when the goblin found her.

Edwina looked at the pieces of fur scattered about the infant. "Well," she said, "now that you've got a good and full belly, you'll be an even juicier meal," and she leaned to pick the baby up.

Wunmor jumped to all fours and hissed at the hobgoblin, then giggled and plopped down on her bottom, playing with a still-moist bone she found at her feet.

"Ack!" squelched the goblin. "Aieee, you's bewitched!" Edwina slapped her spotted head with both hands, making the skin wobble across the skull. "I should'a knowed that's what was off in your waft," she self-admonished, comprehending only now that the odd scent coming from the baby was a combination of human and cat. "I didn't *think* them ears looked right," she snapped. (Edwina hadn't been around humans enough to realize the tail and hair might have been additional clues of something not-quite-right.) The goblin's flappy skin shivered, rolling up and down her back like quaking rungs on a ladder at the thought of how tasty a stew of infant and cat might have been, and she sighed at the realization she'd never know the pleasure. Eating a dead cat was one thing. Being near a live one, even with the human bits, was enough to make her skin crawl. Having a live cat, even if only partially feline, inside her belly was something she didn't want to experiment with.

Hands on her off-kilter hips, Edwina wondered what she should do next. "I'm guessin' those bratty brothers of yours were takin' you to the Moggyfrau to get things sorted out." Her wizened eyes narrowed, "And if they can't get that done, they're mother'll be a bit displeased… assumin' they'd be stupid enough to go home after such a failure, that is." She cackled at the thought of the boys facing the fuming woman.

The bones in her knees cracked and popped in protest as she squatted down to eye-level with Wunmor. "So, the question is… what's do I do with you? Does I help your brothers out and give you back?" The goblin snorted at the idea. "Or does I take you to the Moggyfrau myself?" A vision of cats entered her mind and her crooked spine shuddered. "Or… does I keep ya for my own self?" She mulled whether the cat-baby might be better company than the magpie, and whether she'd be able to keep from eating it long enough to find out. Live cat-ish-ness or not, it was still an infant and, therefore, still barely resistible.

Edwina's thoughts were interrupted by a grumbling that wobbled her belly. "Dang it if I ain't hungry, though."

Wunmor smiled and jumped to her all-fours. She bounded into the grass and bounded back with a rat between her sharp teeth. The rodent had been dead for several days and the decay was well into fermentation.

Edwina's eyes lit up and the corners of her moldering-toothed mouth curled into what she hoped looked like a sweet smile. She queried, "Is there any chance I could have a bit of that?"

The baby spat the dead rat out, directly at the goblin's feet.

Nineteen

"Well, I can't think of no place else that we haven't looked yet," said Dissun, giving one last poke with a long stick deep into a shrub.

"She's gotta be around here somewheres," said Dudderun, chucking one last rock into the bushes before climbing down the short tree where he'd perched for better accuracy.

"What with all of your rock throwin' and my stick jabbin', we'd've sure to've heard somethin' by now," said Dissun.

The two boys looked at the unseelies, piled atop one another, still fast asleep.

"They ain't gonna be no good for a while," said Dudderun

"You have to admit, though," said Dissun, taking a deep breath, "the air's a bit fresher without her around."

"I suppose that *is* a silver linin'," said Dudderun. "But still, we gotta find her. That or don't never try goin' home again."

They thought of what their mother might say, or, more concerning, what she might do if they returned not only without their baby sister repaired to proper babyness, but without the baby whatsoever. Dissun cringed. Dudderun shuddered. Their haunted musings were interrupted by the clanking of a bell.

"What's that danged goat up to?" asked Dissun.

The goat was sniffing at the grass, and when the boys approached, it looked up and shook some fleas from its ears. It belched up some cud and commenced its second breakfast, then, nose twitching, resumed its sniffing.

"Maa!" said the goat, snorting and pawing at the dirt. It looked up at the boys. "Maa!" it said again, then, nose to the ground, trotted away.

Dissun and Dudderun exchanged shrugs, and, having no better options before them, followed the goat. The goat jogged at a brisk pace, leaving the boys behind to follow the sound of its clanking bell. Eventually, the bell stopped clanking. The twins also stopped, not sure which direction to go.

"Maa!"

"That way!" said Dissun, pointing in the direction of the goat's bleating.

When they came upon what they saw, Dissun and Dudderun were surprised, annoyed and, mostly, fascinated.

They were surprised to see the goat looking up to the upper branches of a tree.

They were annoyed that the hobgoblin, Edwina, was there and also looking up to the upper branches of the tree.

They were fascinated when, looking up to the upper branches of the tree, they saw their baby sister in those upper branches. She was laying quite comfortably across a leafy limb, her tail swaying beneath her like a pendulum, gazing down at the small crowd below with large, unblinking eyes.

"What'd you put her up in the tree for?" Dudderun asked the goblin.

"T'wasn't me," she answered. "She did that all by herself."

A few moments passed while everyone looked up at, down at, and over at one another. The goat swallowed its second breakfast and started grazing for its lunch.

"Ya know….," Dissun said to his brother, his eyes attuned on his sister and his hands on his hips, "I'm beginnin' to think we might've been a bit hasty about goin' to the Moggyfrau to fix this. She could be more fun than we'd thunk she'd be."

"That thought was passin' through my mind, too," said Dudderun. "But we gotta choose what's more important. Us havin' some fun, or us survivin' our mum's ire."

"It is a conundrum, that's for sure."

"Why don't you just give'r to me," proposed Edwina. "I'll give'r a nice home."

The boys snorted, and chose not to justify the goblin's suggestion with a reply.

"I don't think we got much choice," said Dissun. "If we're to live beyond the years we are now, we gotta fix'er up so our mum's happy with it."

Dudderun sighed. "I'm afraid you're right," he said, "but how're we gonna get her outta that tree?"

Dissun turned to Edwina. "Do you by any chance know of any old wives' tales about getting' cats outta trees?"

"I think they call someone that's gots a tall ladder," said the goblin. "And, before you ask, no, I ain'tn't gonna climb up 'n get her. She might be lookin' sweet enough now, but there's enough cat in her that there's no trustin' in it. I got enough problems without bein' scratched and bit for the trouble of helpin' the thing."

There was a rustling in the grass, and an unseelie emerged, calling back over its shoulder, "I found 'em!" Some more rustling came towards them from several directions, and the other eleven unseelies also appeared, one by one, and stood next to the first.

"What'd you leave us behind for?" one of them asked.

"We didn't wanna wake you up," said Dudderun.

"And we didn't plan on goin' this far," said Dissun.

The unseelies, following how the goblin and the boys were craning their necks upwards, looked up into the tree.

"Whatchya looking at?" the first unseelie asked, turning its eyes upward. "Oh." It paused, then asked, "What'd you put her up there for?"

"We didn't do it," said Dissun.

"Wasn't me neither," said Edwina.

"Looks like the Moggyfrau's cat hairs gave her all sorts of feline skills," said Dudderun.

"How're you gonna get her down?" asked the unseelie.

"That's what we was just now tryin' to figure out."

The unseelies huddled together, whispering. The boys could make out a few words, such as, "no choice" and "but it's ours" and "we can get some more, the goat's right over there." Finally, twelve green-haired heads nodded in unison, and one of the unseelies stepped forward. "Do you got a bowl or somethin'?" it asked, partly hoping the answer would be 'no'.

"I don't think so…," started Dissun.

"Wait a minute!" Dudderun interrupted him and skipped over to the goat. He took the clanking bell from the animal's collar and brought it back, holding it up like a trophy. "Will this work?"

They dug a small hole in the ground and set the bell upside down in it, and the unseelies, very begrudgingly and with soulful whimpers and sighs, poured the last of the old goat milk from their small jugs into the improvised bowl.

Wunmor looked from goblin to brother to fairy, and jumped down from the tree. After emptying the bowl, she sat and licked her small hands and cleaned her whiskers with them.

"Aw, ain't she a cute one!" Edwina cooed. Then, remembering who and what she was, looked to her feet and kicked at a clump of grass, grumbling something about despicable cats.

Dudderun kneeled down and reached for his sister. "If I can just pick you up," he said, as Wunmor watched his every move, " we can head on towards the Moggyfrau and – "

Wunmor, with her tiny and sharp claws extended, swiped at her brother.

"Ouch!" Dudderun yanked his hand back.

Wunmor jumped to all fours, hissed, giggled, and ran off into the grass.

"Don't let her get away!" shouted Dissun, running after his sister, with his brother, the goblin and the twelve unseelies behind him.

The goat looked up, grinding a mouthful of grass between its molars. It shook its head, enjoying the lack of a bell clanking on its neck. A family of fleas rose from one ear and flitted to the other. Brown, slotted nanny eyes watched the disturbances in the grass, with the baby veering off to one side and everyone else continuing straight ahead.

"Maa!" said the goat.

It curled its legs beneath itself, and lay down to take a nap.

Twenty

A top her thatched roof, the Moggyfrau, surrounded by dozens of cats, was watching the sun go down. Her meditations were interrupted when one of them said, "Will you look at that?"

Turning to the direction the cat was looking, the tiny witch keened her eyes across the hills and spotted the strange group making their way towards her house. "It's that stinking goblin again!" she said. "But this time she's not riding in a tree. Looks like she's on a goat instead."

"Should we go to greet her?" said the black feline, wicking the tip of its tail sharply back and forth.

"Naw," said the Moggyfrau, "this time we'll stay right here and let her come to us. Might be fun to see her bein' surrounded by my precious kitties."

"Something's coming our way," the calico sitting on top of the clean dishes called out from the kitchen window below.

"We see's it," the Moggyfrau called back. "Let everyone know we've got company." Then she added, with a snicker, "Tell them it's that Edwina goblin."

"Sun's about to set," said Dudderun. "You sure it's safe to visit a witch in the twilight?"

"Who's to say that's any worse than sleepin' out here where a goblin might eat you when you's asleep?" Dissun looked at the hobgoblin standing a safe distance away. Safe for them, and for herself.

"Hmph!" Edwina snorted. "You're too old," she grumbled under her breath, "we goblins only eats the new ones. They's softer and juicier."

The twins were standing on a grassy knoll with one small hill between them and the home of the Moggyfrau. Beside them stood the goat with a row of twelve unseelies sitting on its straight and boney back.

"Well," said Dissun, "we'd ought to not dilly-dally."

Dudderun nodded and the group made their way down the knoll, across the next hill, and in no time found themselves approaching the front yard of the Moggyfrau's house.

"Aieee…" Edwina groaned, "I can't do this." Her skin was covered in goosebumps from the top of her spotted head to the tips of the claws on her gravelly toes – goblin goosebumps. "There's too many of 'em. I can't abide bein' anywhere near a live cat, and especially not a gaggle of 'em!" Her scrawny legs began to shift sideways.

"Don't you even *think* about runnin' away," Dissun scolded the goblin. "We wouldn't be in this here predicament if it wasn't for you."

"What're you talkin' about?" Edwina sneered. "You're the ones who got her changed outta what she's supposed to be."

"Yeah, but we'd still have her if you hadn't gone and tried to steal her for your supper," said Dudderun.

"I wasn't gonna eat her," said the goblin. "I was gonna make her my apprentice."

"That was only after you decided not to eat her," said Dissun.

"Well," said Edwina, "she wouldn't make much of an apprentice if she was in my belly, would she?"

Dudderun pondered for a moment, then said, "That don't make no sense."

"You could'a kept chasin' her," said Edwina.

"She was too quick," said Diddun. "Like a cat."

"We's had to come to the witch fer help," said Dudderun. "Weren't no choice about it."

"Maa!" said the goat.

"See, the goat agrees," said Edwina.

"Maa!"

"Hah! She's agreein' with us," said Dissun.

"Maa!"

"She's not agreeing with either of you," said one of the unseelies. "She's trying to tell you to shut up. The Moggyfrau's standing on her porch, waitin' for you."

"Maa!"

"Thank you, ma'am," Dissun said, remembering the miniscule smattering of manners his mother had been able to get into his head.

"Would you like some sugar? I'd offer cream, but that's saved for my kitties."

"No, thank you," said Dudderun, who had absorbed nearly the same amount knowledge regarding manners as his brother. He sneezed.

They were sitting at a round table not quite in the middle of the living room of the Moggyfrau's home, each with a cup of hot tea in front of them. It was also the kitchen, the bedroom, and the closet, because there was only one room. Several cats had perched themselves along the mantle above the large fireplace, and many more were sitting and lying on the rug in front of it. There was a calico cat on top of the dishes in the sink. More cats, of every color and hair length, most with tails and a few without, lay across the floor, out through the door and covering the porch. Except for the narrow pathway, where they'd left room for the Moggyfrau and the boys to walk, it looked as if the place had been carpeted with cats, inside and out. A sleek black cat sat in the middle of the table.

Every feline was watching Dissun and Dudderun, except for the calico. It was looking out the window, watching the goblin sitting on a rock a short distance away. The unseelies sat next to the goblin with full jugs of old goat milk, and the goat, feeling refreshed after a good milking, was nibbling at the grass around the rock.

"So, you're telling me the cat hairs worked, but now you're mother's not too pleased about it." The Moggyfrau climbed into a chair that faced the twins. Her round body wobbled a bit before settling in place, and her feet dangled high above the floor. She took a sip of her tea, scrunched her nose, dug into her pocket, sprinkled something into the brew, took another sip, and smiled. "I'm not sure what you expect me to do about that."

"We was hopin' you could put her back the way she was," said Dissun.

"The baby, that is," Dudderun said, not wanting there to be any confusion, "not our mum."

"Moggybairn," said the black cat on the table.

"Huh?" said Dissun.

"It's not a baby anymore," the cat said, haughty boredom oozing from every word. "It's a Moggybairn."

"What's that?" said Dudderun.

"Moggyfrau, cat lady," the cat said. "Cat baby, Moggybairn."

The boys thought for a moment, then one of them said, "Don't matter what she's called now. We need her back the ways she was on account of our mum wantin' things to be that way."

The cat stared at the boys, as if deciding whether they were worth any further education, then, concluding they weren't, stretched, yawned a wide yawn that showed every sharp white tooth, and laid itself across the table.

"What do you got to barter?" asked the witch, her dandelion head nodding as she looked back and forth between the two boys.

Dissun and Dudderun exchanged looks, but said nothing.

"Well," said the tiny witch, "you can't just come and ask for something without having something to trade for it." Her body teetered to one side, and she scooched herself back in place. "You see, last time we had a trade. You helped me out of a bind, and I gave you something to help make your baby sister more enjoyable. Are you saying she ain't no fun now?"

"Oh, no," said Dissun. "She's more fun than ever we could've imagined. But it's our mum."

"We wish we could just keep her this way," Dudderun said, "there's no end to the thinkin' of what fun we could get into with her being like she is now. But our mum, she ain't so happy about it."

"And we can't go back home again until we've set things back like they was before," said Dissun.

"What about that bag of eyes," said the black cat. "The one the goblin carries on her belt?"

"Ah, well there's an idea," said the Moggyfrau. "If you can get that for us, I'll see what I can do for you and your sister."

"We'd have no problem givin' that to you," said Dissun.

"But it ain't ours to give," finished Dudderun.

"Well, then, I expect it's time for you to be on your way," said the Moggyfrau.

Dissun and Dudderun looked to each other.

"I suppose it's worth a try," said one.

"I suppose so," said the other.

"Nope!" Edwina crossed her arms.

"But wasn't you gonna see her about them anyways?" asked Dissun.

"That was on my terms," the goblin raised her crooked nose to the air and jutted her pointy chin out. "I ain't doin' nothing on her terms." She cracked the warted lid of one eye open and looked sideways at the boys. "What's in it for me?"

"Don't trust her, is what we says," called out an unseelie, falling off the rock as it spoke. The eleven other unseelies laughed raucously, and two more rolled off the rock. The three fairies on the ground pulled themselves to the side of the rock so they could lean back on the stone, and continued swigging from their jugs.

"Don't trust the witch nor this here hobgoblin," said one of the three.

"Don't trust nobody," said another, raising its jug high.

"You can trust us!" said another.

"Oh, well, of course you can trust *us*. Just don't go trustin' nobody else."

The first unseelie to fall off the rock fell sideways, rolled on its back, mumbling, "…frog eyes… goblin eyes… likho eyes… cat eyes…." And it began to snore, protectively tucking its jug in tight against its skinny body.

Dissun and Dudderun grinned at the ideas they were having. A cat who'd been sitting on the porch watching them with its night-enabled eyes, hissed and puffed up all its hairs on end and run into the house at the sight.

"

Twenty-One

"**W**hat do you mean, a *compromise?*" the Moggyfrau said. "Witches don't compromise."

"Well, then, we can call it a bargain," said Dissun.

"A barter of sorts," added Dudderun.

"You'll get the bag of eyes for me," the witch said, slowly, making sure she understood the agreement she might be entering into, "and I give it back, but I get to keep the likho's eyes."

"After you cleans it up!" Edwina shouted from the rock. Goblins have very good hearing, and she was listening closely, making sure she understood the agreement she might be entering into as well.

"Yes, yes…," the witch waved a shooing hand at the hobgoblin. "And you won't be comin' back for them?"

"They's the likho's eyes," said Edwina. "Don't matter to me what happens to them." She wasn't really sure that it wouldn't, eventually, matter to her. But she decided she could figure that bit out later.

"And, after you've got them eyes and she's got her bag back, all cleaned up and full of her mum's and grandmum's and so-on's eyes," said Dudderun, "you'll do whatever needs doin' to set the baby straight."

"Remind me again why I'm doing that for you?" asked the Moggyfrau.

"'Cause on account of us brokerin' the arrangement," said Dissun. "If it wasn't for us, you'd be getting' nothin' and the goblin out there'd still have an old mucked up bag."

"And what will the goblin be giving you for the brokering?" asked the witch.

"We'll get an I-owes-you from her," Dudderun said, then called out the door, "ain't that right?"

"Yes, yes, yes…," Edwina answered, grumbling something afterwards which the boys chose not to hear.

"Hmmm…," pondered the witch. "I appear to be doin' more than either of the three of you. Seems I should be getting a bit more."

"What're ya thinkin'?" asked Dissun.

"I want that goat."

"The goat?" said Dudderun.

"You got it!" yelled Edwina.

"What?"

"Wait a minute!"

"Ain't we got no say in it?"

The last several comments came from the unseelies who, upon hearing the Moggyfrau's proposal, were suddenly, soberly, awake. Except for the sleeping fairy who muttered, "Did someone say somethin' about the goat?" Then it burped, and fell back asleep.

"You can't do that!" said one of the fairies.

"We's got an agreement," said another.

"Your mother'll miss the old nanny," said a third, followed by shushes and *don't say that* and *she'll be glad it's gone* from the other fairies.

"They're right," said Dissun. "We'll be back to doin' our own chores."

"And they're also right that our mum won't miss the old goat's aroma none," said Dudderun.

"Sorry," Dissun called out to the unseelies, "but we's gotta do what we's gotta do."

"Maybe we should've asked the Moggyfrau if'n we could've spent the night before headin' home," said Dudderun. "It's mighty dark out here."

"I dunno," said Dissun, "don't you remember our mum tellin' us about the potential horrors of sleepin' overnight under a witch's roof? We'd've been shoved into the oven for sure."

"I didn't see no oven in that kitchen."

"Well, then, she'd've put us in that pot hangin' over the fire."

"You think the both of us could've fit in there?"

"Might could, if we got squeezed real good."

They walked a bit farther, trying not to trip over rocks.

"At least it's a full moon out tonight," said Dudderun. "Maybe we won't get too lost."

"Don't matter none," said Dissun. "We can't go home until we find Wunmor anyways."

"Maybe she'll find us instead."

"She might. And hopefully it'll be before any critters up and eats us."

"What kinds of critters do you think there are?" Dudderun looked over his shoulder.

"Well, there's sure to be somethin' and it's sure to be wantin' to eat us."

"I wonder if it'd take one bite or two."

"Depends on what it is that's eatin' us, I suppose."

They paused their conversation for a bit, then Dudderun spoke up.

"Them danged Unseelies are sure to be holdin' a grudge, that's gonna be for sure."

"Mighty rude of them to just go marchin' off like that. They could've at least stayed with us, you know, to scare off the things that'll be wantin' to eat us."

"You think that Edwina goblin'll keep her side of the I-owes-you?"

"I guess we'll be findin' out sometime in the future."

"Assumin', of course, that we don't get all eaten up before we's can take advantage of it."

The night grew darker, and the grass grew taller.

Strange sounds surrounded the boys, and they decided it might be best to curtail their discussion and continue in silence until they could see that there was nothing dangerously nearby to hear them.

As they walked, they listened to the croaking of toads, the chirping of crickets, several whoops and a couple of howls that made them quicken their pace, and, wafting through it all, so hushed they weren't sure if it was real or their imaginations, they heard hissing followed by giggles, and they let that final set of sounds guide them in the direction they would be going.

Twenty-Two

To Wunmor, the field of grass promised adventure. She dashed through the yellowed stalks, crawled between green blades, and pounced on rocks that she decided were dangerous monsters. She hissed at bugs and worms, and giggled at the butterflies that dipped and drifted just above her reach.

Farther and farther she went, deeper and deeper into the meadow, until she came out on the other side where the forest began.

She looked from the grass to the trees. In most places, fields of grass gradually thin and blend into a forest, and the trees gradually grow dense as you enter the woods. But this forest and grass did not behave that way. Instead, it was as if they'd come to an agreement and drawn a line of boundary, delineating which side was whose. The grass stopped, and the trees grew tall and thick, standing together.

Some people – most people, and even most everything – would view this as a border that needed some consideration before crossing. However, Wunmor, being young and happy and half-cat, continued into the forest with no deliberation. In her opinion, of course she should. The grass had been an entertaining diversion, and this change of scenery hinted at even more adventure and who-knows-what tiny critters to pounce upon. And there was the added benefit of trees to climb and sharpen her small claws on.

Wunmor pranced from the grass to the trees, spotted an odd-shaped stick, and dashed behind a shrub, envisioning herself as a fearless hunter stalking its prey.

It was growing dark, but that didn't matter to the Moggybairn, with her slitted cat-eyes. When she grew bored with attacking sticks and rocks, she climbed a tree, scaling its sides up to a high branch. The woods were too dense to see any distance, but the trees were close enough that she could easily leap from one to another. She jumped from branch to branch, from tree to tree, until she was deep into the forest where the trees were so thick she couldn't see the stars or even the moon with its full and round belly. She wasn't afraid, though, because she was young and half-cat, and she followed the sounds of crickets and birds that hunted in the night. And, at first faintly but steadily growing, there was the sound of voices.

Wunmor thought to herself, *I will hunt whatever is making the talking noises, and I will* eat *them where they stand.*

Wunmor giggled at the fun she was having. She took a deep breath and fluffed the fur on her tail so every hair stood on-end, and she tiptoed towards the voices. She came to a clearing where a small fire was surrounded by a strange assortment of trees that sat on rocks around the flaming pit, she climbed to a high branch and perched where she could watch.

"Your curses are like your stew. All broth, no meat," said one of the trees.

"And you can never be sure what's in them," said another.

One of the trees was a pine, its long arms covered with needles, and its head and hands made of cone. Another was an oak, with scaly gray bark and pointed leaves. There was a tall one, with a thick red trunk, its head high above the others. A willow sat and cried, wiping its incessant tears with its drooping branches. There didn't seem to be any particular reason for it to be crying, and the other trees around it were giving it looks of annoyance. But none of that made any difference. The crying continued, quietly, persistently. A stocky shrub was near the oak. It had round leaves and little red berries, and was so stout Wunmor wasn't sure if it was sitting or standing.

All of these trees sat in a half-circle.

Across from them sat a dark tree with a jagged head that looked like it had been burned in a fire, a trunk that bifurcated into two legs that ended in thick roots, long branches for arms and twigs for fingers. Its eyes were the eyes of a frog. In the crook of a limb nestled a happy, pink pig.

The full moon was high up into the sky when Dissun and Dudderun came across a fenced yard of neatly-mowed lawn encircling a small house made of red brick. A tendril of smoke coming from the chimney told them someone was probably inside.

"What do you think?" said Dissun. "You think it's safe?"

"Can't tell from here," said Dudderun. "But it might be worth a try, seein' as how we ain't gettin' nowhere otherwise."

"We could get ourselves eaten."

"Could. And that wouldn't be too good." Dudderun paused in thought, then said, "But if it's just one of us that gets eaten, and it's you, I promise to tell our mum it wasn't your fault."

"I would be obliged for that," said Dissun, "and if it's you that gets eaten I'll do the same."

The boys nodded. They weren't grinning. They hadn't grinned for quite some time.

"Do you see a gate anywhere?"

"No. As far as I can tell, there ain't none."

"Well, then, here goes nothin'," said Dudderun, and he hoisted himself over the fence. Dissun followed his brother, and they cautiously made their way towards the porch, which was also made of red brick. About ten paces in, the front door of the house slammed open and an old man in baggy overalls came bounding out.

"You sodding little whippersnappers!" The man walked with a stick, which he pointed at the boys as he yelled at them. "You get off my lawn!"

Dissun and Dudderun froze. The only other person they'd known who was near the age of this old man was their grandfather, and, while he could be cantankerous, this level of crankiness was something they'd never witnessed from him. It was possible their mother had displayed annoyance near this level, but she would never had been so worked up over a lawn. She saved her exasperation for other, more important things.

The boys weren't sure what to do.

"Look at what you're doing!" yammered the old man. "You're crushing the grass with your feet, and leaving big footprints everywhere."

"We're a bit confused," said Dissun to the man. "What is it that you're wantin' us to do?"

"Get off my lawn!" The old man accentuated each word with a sharp jab of his stick.

"But," said Dudderun, looking around at his feet, "you seem to be bothered by the fact that our feet're leavin' footprints, and, as I'm sure my brother will agree, it don't seem possible to accord with your wishes without makin' more of 'em."

Dissun nodded vigorously.

"Blast it!" the old man snarled. He turned and headed back towards the house. "Walk on your tippytoes!" he growled over his shoulder, then grumbled more words the boys understood the meaning of even if they couldn't make them out.

"Which direction would you like us to go?" asked Dissun.

"We're halfway across the lawn," said Dudderun. "Would you prefer we go back and add to the damage already done, or try our best to complete our way across?"

The man stopped. He didn't look back. "You're here this far," he said, his face towards the sky above his white head, his eyes fixed on the round, full moon. "You might as well finish your dangberned, dagnabbited tramplin' and come on into the house."

"Did'ya see that?" Dissun whispered to his brother, nudging him with an elbow.

"The pointed ears and long nose?" said Dudderun. "I surely did."

"I'm not so sure of the safety in followin' him," said Dissun.

"But we still got the same problem of not knowin' which way to go if'n we want to find our sister," said Dudderun.

"Not to mention he might just get more mad at us if we forget our manners and take off without a howdy-bye."

"If'n he eats us, it won't matter which way we go because there'll be no more goin'."

"He's mighty cranky, but d'ya really think he'd eat us?"

"I'm not sure I'd put anything past any whatnot tonight."

"Get on over here!" the old man barked from the porch.

The boys shrugged, nodded an unspoken *It's been a fun life,* and raised their arms to balance themselves as they walked on the tips of their toes across the grass. When they reached the porch, they flattened their feet and their toes eeked with joy.

The old man opened the door and walked into the house. He didn't hold the door open for the boys, and it slammed shut behind him. They hesitated, then heard him yell, "Well, are you comin' in or not?"

Twenty-Three

A warm fire below the chimney. A large chair with
pillows. A table with plates and maybe what was left
of dinner, and a mug filled with whatever an old man might
drink at this time of night. A kitchen full of cups and dishes.
Pictures on the wall. A warm coat hanging on a hook near
the door, and a pair of heavy boots beneath them. Lanterns
strategically placed so as to provide ample light throughout
the room.

All of these were things that might be expected within a
red brick house with a neat lawn around it.

All of these were things that were *not* within *this* red brick
house, regardless of the neat lawn. Except for the fire. There
was an exceptionally large and warm fire below the chimney.
The only other thing in this house was a rocking chair made
of wood, with scratches and bites along its legs and armrests.

On the hearth rested a simple basket of apples and carrots and several small loaves of bread. One of the loaves was mostly eaten, and apple cores could be seen among the burning logs in the fire. There was one window to the house, positioned so the moon could be seen when it reached the horizon.

"Sit wherever you want," the old man said, sitting in the chair and apparently ignoring the fact that there was nowhere else to sit but on the floor. "But not too close to me. You humans are an untrustworthy lot."

Dissun and Dudderun sat cross-legged a respectable, polite and even distance between the rocking chair and the fire. Trying not to stare, they couldn't help but notice the walls were etched with what looked like scratches from the long claws of very large paws.

"I can't say as I blame you for not trusting humans," said Dudderun. "Our mum tells us the same."

"But she usually says not to trust other *people*," Dissun said. He looked at the old man. "After all, we're all human… *aren't we?*" His voice quaked a little, and the last two words had a bit of a squeak to them.

The old man snorted, jumped from the chair and began pacing back and forth. "Only when the moon is full." His feet were bare and his toenails dug into the floor with each turn. He man stopped his pacing and stared deep into the fire. "I'm a vulfusgrump." The words came out in a growl.

"A vuffsuffgr – " started Dudderun.

"*Vulfusgrump!*" the man snapped.

"I'm sorry, that's for sure," said Dudderun. "But I don't think I've ever heard of such a thing before."

"Nor me," said Dissun.

"You've heard of a werewolf?" said the old man, still staring at the flames.

The boys grew nervous.

"No," said the old man. "I'm not one of those."

"You ain't gonna eats us?"

"No," the man said, "leastwise, not during the full moon, when I'm in this… condition."

"So, you're *not* a werewolf?" Dissun scooted a bit farther from the old man and a bit closer to his brother.

"No. Like I just told you. I'm a vulfusgrump."

"We're sorry," said Dissun, "but we don't know what that is."

"You've heard how a man can turn into a werewolf if he's bitten by a wolf?"

The boys nodded, wide-eyed.

"A vulfusgrump is a wolf that's been bitten by an old man. Vulfus is an old-world word for wolf."

Dissun nudged his brother. "I think I remember hearin' grandpa usin' that word."

"So, you're…" Dudderun tried to figure out what he was hearing.

"I am a wolf." The man turned away from the fire and went back to sit in the rocking chair. "One day, a few years back, the moon was full and I was out hunting when I came up upon a farm. There were chickens running loose, and, I thought to myself, the farm wouldn't miss just a couple of them."

"I dunno about that," said Dissun. "Our mum counts the chickens every time she feeds 'em. And if any's missin' my brother and me hear about it until we find 'em."

The old man nodded. "That's what I found out. I'd barely gotten one between my teeth when out came this old man, running up at me with a stick. Yelling and shouting…" a snarl came to his lips at the memory, and his teeth clenched tight.

"So, what happened?" asked Dudderun.

"What do you *think* happened? I dropped the chicken and tried to run away. But he caught up to me and started whacking me with his stick. I grabbed the stick in my teeth and tossed it aside, and I tried again to run away. But that old man grabbed me. And he *bit me!*" The vulfusgrump pulled up one pantleg and showed them the scar in the form of a set of human teeth. They weren't perfect teeth. They were crooked, and a few were missing. It reminded them of what an apple looked like after their grandfather had taken a bite out of it.

The boys didn't know what to say, so they said nothing.

"If a vulfus, a wolf, gets bitten on a full moon," the vulfusgrump continued, "every full moon after that they turn into whatever it was that bit them. So, ever since then, when the moon is full I turn into an old man. He was a real curmudgeon, so that's what *I* become. But, and this is a promise I will see fulfilled, that old man *will* get his comeuppance." He paused, then added, quietly, "Sorry about the lawn thing."

"Oh, that's alright," said Dissun. "Considerin' the circumstances, it's completely understandable."

"You couldn't help yourself," said Dudderun. "It was the moon that done it."

The vulfusgrump smiled. It was a strange smile, what with his unusually long nose and white, pointed teeth, but it was a friendly one. "My name is Aldbrecht, by the way."

"Pleased to meet you Mr. Aldbrecht," said Dissun.

"Just Aldbrecht."

"Pleased to meet you Aldbrecht," said Dissun. "I'm Dissun and this here's my brother Dudderun."

"Odd names," said the old man.

"It was our grandpa's doin'," said Dudderun.

"So," said Aldbrecht, "do you want to tell me why you're out here, perilously close to the Goblin Forest, in the middle of the night, on a full moon no less?"

"We're lookin' for our sister," said Dissun.

"She's a Moggybairn, and we's gots ta find her and make her back to normal and bring her home to our mum," said Dudderun.

"And if'n we can't do that, we might just as well keep on goin' down whatever road we find and seeks our fortunes," said Dissun.

"And you thought I might be able to help you?" said the vulfusgrump.

"We didn't know it'd be you," said Dissun, "but we was hopin' whoever we found in this here house might be able to give us some guidance."

"What was that you just said about us bein' perilously close to a Goblin Forest?" asked Dudderun.

Twenty-Four

*E*dwina wished she had her pink pig with her. Riding the swine not only would make things go faster, it would also relieve the tired, sinewy muscles in her skinny legs. She wished the magpie was along as well, so she could have someone to complain to. But both of them, the pig and the magpie, had gone home with the likho. So, under the full moon, with groaning legs and unwitnessed bellyaching, she stomped through the grassy meadow.

The hobgoblin knew she was going in the right direction. Her pointy nose could easily detect and follow the Moggybairn's distinct aroma

The scents of bratty boys and wolves drifted by, and Edwina stopped walking.

"Hmm...," she thought aloud, "this is a bit of a quandary. As I sees it, I've got two options afore me. I could follow the cretin boys and tells 'em which ways the baby is, thereby fulfillin' my I-owes-you, but there's a wolf about and I mights find meself bein' its dinner if I goes that way." Her long mouth drooped at the ends and she crossed her arms, cupping her warted chin in one hand. "Or I could keep goin' as I been goin' and find the baby." The drooping lips curled up into a strange smile. "And, who's to say what happens if I never come across them imbeciles again? I'll have me the newborn brat." She shivered a little at the thought of the baby being part-cat, but quickly set that thought aside. "And I'd be *obligated* to take it into my care, wouldn't I?"

Edwina sniffed the air, securing the direction from which each of the scents was coming. When she was sure of the origins, she turned on her bony heels and followed the aroma of the Moggybairn, which was in a completely different direction from that of the boys.

The goblin didn't mind that she was heading towards the Goblin Forest. It was one of the few places, other than her own cozy goblin cave, where she would feel right at home.

"Will you stop that incessant weeping?" the Oak groused at the tearful tree.

"I can't help it," the Willow answered. "It's what I am."

"You could choose to be something else," said the Pine. "We're likhos and we can pick any tree we want to be."

"Like old Burnt here," laughed the Chokeberry shrub. "You just set your toes in a field of cow dung when you're turning, and look what you can be!" Berries fell from the shrub, it was laughing so hard.

"Kind of like its stew." The Oak laughed, acorns falling to the ground around it.

"And its curses," snickered the Chokeberry, catching its breath.

"I'm too sad to even think about it," said the Willow.

"You know I can't help it," snapped the likho named Burnt. Few people knew its name, and it preferred to keep things that way as it was rather embarrassing how it had been earned. "How was I to know the field was full of fresh manure?" It closed its frog eyes and scratched behind the ears of the pink pig sleeping in the crook of its arm.

"That's enough of that," the tallest of the trees, the Redwood, spoke. Its voice was low, earthy and old.

The laughing and snickering, and even the weeping, stopped.

"We're not here to make fun of each other," said the Redwood. "We're here for a nice family picnic."

"Isn't it Burnt's turn to be the host?" asked the Pine.

"Should be," giggled the Chokeberry, "but since it knocked down its own house we have to go alfresco."

"Besides," sniggered the Oak, "we wouldn't want to end up being cursed on to of having empty stomachs."

"I assure you," groused Burnt, "there have been good reasons for everything."

"Stop." The Redwood, quietly but with little patience. "Burnt brought us some salad – "

"More like uncooked stew minus the meat," the Chokeberry muttered under its breath. It stopped and looked at its roots when the Redwood gave it a sideways glare.

"Let's just try and enjoy our dinner," said the Redwood. It picked up a tomato, and squeezed it. The tomato burst open, sending bits of red organic flesh across the face of the tall tree.

"I don't think you're supposed to squeeze them," said the Pine.

"A Goblin Forest?" Dissun's eyes were wider than they'd ever been.

"Our mum told us about that," said Dudderun, with equally wide eyes, "but we figured it was fairytales."

"Yes," said the vulfusgrump, "the Goblin Forest. And, no, it's not a fairytale."

"And that's where we'll find our sister?" Dissun said.

"It might not be as bad as you think," said the vulfusgrump. "The trees are likhos. Goblin-trees. Well, about half of them anyway. And likhos don't tend to eat people."

"One of 'em tried to eat us," said Dudderun.

"Yeah," said Dissun, "but, to be fair, that may have been more on account of it bein' payback."

"Payback for what happened when it wanted to eats our mum."

"That's true," said Dissun, and he turned to the vulfusgrump. "We ain't so sure we can trust they won't wanna eats us on sight."

"They're less likely to have you for dinner than, say, the hobgoblins who live in the forest among them."

"Hobgoblins?"

"Like that Edwina goblin?"

"All's she can think about is eatin' our baby sister."

"But not *you*," said the vulfusgrump. "You're too old and chewy for a hobgoblin's taste."

"You have a good point," said Dudderun. "But there's sure to be lots of 'em, and they's greedy ol' things."

"Don't seem as if we got much choice," Dissun said to his brother. "Our sister's in there. And whether the purpose is to save our hides or hers, the goal's the same. We gots ta get her outta there."

Aldbrecht stared into the fire, mumbling something to himself. Then he groaned and, turning to the boys, said, "As soon as the moon sets, and I'm back to being my regular wolf self, we can go in the morning and I will guide you."

Dissun and Dudderun grinned their grins that, for once, didn't unnerve the other person in the room with them.

"You will?" they exclaimed in unison.

"The moon's full for one more night after this, so I don't have anything else to do for at least another day. I might as well accompany you." Aldbrecht said.

It was at that moment that Dissun's stomach growled uncomfortably, and it was answered by an equally uncomfortable growl from the stomach belonging to

Dudderun. The two boys tried not to look at the basket of bread and apples and carrots.

"Would it be a ridiculous question to ask if you two are hungry?" said Aldbrecht.

"We've not eaten in some time," said Dissun.

"Our mum gave us some sammiches when she sent us off," said Dudderun, "but that was yesterday. Or maybe the day before."

Aldbrecht nodded towards the basket. "Help yourselves," he said.

Not needing to be told twice, Dudderun scooted closer to the basket. He stuffed a carrot in his mouth, and grabbed an apple and a loaf of bread, one for each hand. Dissun did the same.

Between chews and gulps and smacks, Dissun asked, "How'd you get this food?" He and his brother had noticed that it wasn't what they'd expected a wolf would have for dinner.

"It shows up on the doorstep," said the vulfusgrump. "I suspect the Hogboons."

"We's heard of 'em," said Dissun. "They's not so bad, as far as goblins go."

"Mum always did say they was one of the nicer ones," said Dudderun.

"Perhaps," said Aldbrecht. "But it's probably also so I'm not hungry when the full moon's done. Benevolence with a bit of self-preservation."

"Sounds smart," said Dissun. "We'd rather your belly was full so's we don't look too tasty to you when you're back to your rightful self."

"I'm not sure there's enough seasonings around to make you two appear tasty, even on a ravenous stomach," said Aldbrecht.

"Well, whatever it is we're doin' to make us unsavory to your taste-buds, we're sure to want to keep on doin' it," said Dudderun.

"Not to mention," said Aldbrecht, offhandedly, "it's bad luck to eat anything that has a curse hanging over its head."

"A curse?"

"On us?"

"Who says we gots a curse?"

"I can sense it," said Aldbrecht.

"Mum never told us about no curse."

Twenty-Five

*E*dwina was so intent on following her nose, she didn't hear the rustling in the grass around her. By the time she was aware, it was too late.

"Have you found her yet?" said the unseelie, hopping out from the grass in front of her, followed by eleven others exactly like the first.

"No, I haven't," said Edwina. She stepped sideways to get around the unseelies, and continued walking.

"We wanna come with you," said the unseelie. The twelve fairies trotted after the goblin.

"Why?"

"We want that goat back," said another of the unseelies.

"We don't know how to do that, but helpin' to retrieve the baby seems like a good start," said another.

"And makin' sure you don't eat her," said a third, then quickly added, "No offense meant."

"None taken," said Edwina. "Eatin' that baby'd be somethin' I'd be delighted to do. But I gots to get at her afore them boys do and they return her to that – *phfwaat!* – " she spat, " – woman."

The Moggyfrau was on top of her house, sitting on the thatched roof, as she always did on nights when the moon was full. She could see in the dark with the same acuity as the multitude of cats around her. She could also see very, very far into the distance. And what she saw was the Moggybairn running through the meadow and into the forest.

"I have a regret," she said to the black cat sitting next to her.

"Such is the flaw of not being a cat," the feline replied. It licked a paw and wiped behind one ear.

"I shouldn't've let her go," said the Moggyfrau. "I've got no need for an old goat, and that tyke is one of us now. It should be upon me to be carin' for her."

"Her mother might disagree."

"Her mother put that baby in the care of her bumbling brothers, and I don't know about you but I wouldn't call that carin' too ferociously."

The cat looked at the tiny woman. "Underestimation is a troublesome thing."

"That's right!" said the Moggyfrau. "And I'm a wee bit tired of bein' underestimated."

"That's not exactly what I meant," said the cat, but the witch chose not to hear.

"Time to go," said the Moggyfrau. She stood up and raised her small hand, and the broom obediently flew into her grasp.

Every cat in, on and around the Moggyfrau's house gathered together. Thirteen of them jumped on the broom with her. The sleek, black cat sat at the tip of the broom, in front of the witch.

The Moggyfrau bent her little legs, pushed off from the ground, and flew across the sky with the horde cats effortlessly running below, following her.

"A pretty chain," the magpie said, pulling the jewelry into the pile of baubles, "and a piece of gold," it reached out a foot and grabbed a ring that had rolled from the mound. "Ahhh…," it sighed, tucking its feet under itself and settling into its nest of trinkets.

The cave was quiet.

"Wock! It's too quiet!" squawked the magpie. "I can't stand it!"

The magpie skipped to the mouth of the cave. The night sky was bright with the full moon, but the bird knew it wouldn't last. Eventually, the moon would set behind the mountains and it would be as dark as its corvid feathers.

"Woot!" said the magpie, having second thoughts. "As I've said before, we magpies aren't night birds. I can stand the quiet for one more night. That hobgoblin'll still be out there tomorrow. And that ludicrous pig, too." It hopped back to its nest and went to sleep.

Twenty-Six

*P*erched in the tree, high enough to not be seen but low enough to hear, Wunmor learned several things.

She learned that the likhos were goblins who looked like trees, and that they didn't normally eat humans. Not normally. But it wasn't a rule, and sometimes, for a likho, a human could make a tasty stew if you boiled them long enough.

She learned that, unlike other goblins who could only curse *at* you, a likho could put a curse *on* you. There was a big difference, apparently.

She learned that one of the likhos, the one that looked dark and burned, and that they called Burnt, had put a curse on her brothers, and also on a bag containing eyes. Wunmor remembered seeing a small pouch on Edwina's belt, and she thought, *I think I'd like to take a look inside that bag sometime.*

The Moggybairn decided that likhos would be the first things in her newborn world that she would not like. Everything else had been fun, and interesting, and delightful. But, as far as she could tell, the likhos were none of those things.

Wunmor, in her growing dislike of these particular goblins, stretched her claws and dug them into the branch where she was sitting. And that's when she learned one more thing. She learned that the tree in which she was perched was also a likho.

"We've got a spy in our midst," said the Pine, as it grabbed Wunmor's tail and stretched out its branch, holding her out for all to see.

"What *is* that thing?" cried the Willow.

"It's not a goblin, that much is for sure," said the Oak. "Look how puny it is!"

"It almost… smells…," the Chokeberry's leaves rattled as it sniffed the air, "… almost human. But not quite."

"Well, it's obviously not human," said the Oak. "Look at those ears and tail. Those aren't human things."

"Could be a Tatzelwurm. I've heard there's some that's migrated down from the mountains."

"Naw, the head's close to being Tatzelwurm, but this one's got arms and legs. What you're thinking of would be more like a snake from the neck on down."

Burnt said nothing, but it was thinking.

"I know what it is!" said the Pine, leaning down its long neck of a trunk. "It's a Moggybairn."

"The Moggyfrau has a child?"

"This can't be a child of the Moggyfrau. It's small, but not *that* small."

"Well, it's something akin to her," said the Pine. "Those parts that aren't human are cat, and that makes it Moggy-ish."

Wunmor didn't cry. Or hiss. Or giggle. She let herself hang by the tail, and gazed at the likhos, each one in turn.

"I don't like how the thing's looking at us," wept the Willow. "Somebody make it stop."

"It's very unsettling," said the Oak.

Wunmor narrowed her eyes, sharpening her gaze, ignoring the slow swaying back and forth as she swung like a pendulum.

"I don't know if I would do that, if I were you," said the Oak. "If it's anything near like the Moggyfrau, you could end up sorry."

The Chokeberry nervously rustled its berries. "Whether it's a grievance from the Moggybairn, if that's what this thing is, or from the Moggyfrau, if she's at all involved, it doesn't forebode well to swing her back and forth like that."

Wunmor let a little bit of a grin seep across her mouth, and her two longest fangs bared themselves.

"It's really creeping me out," wailed the Willow. "Make it stop."

"Argh!" Out of patience, the Redwood snatched the Moggybairn from the twig-fingers of the Pine.

Wunmor knew an opportunity when she saw one – she was, after all, her brothers' sister – and in the speck of the moment between when she was released by her captor and when she was seized by the Redwood, she flared her tail into a bottlebrush, revealed her mouthful of sharp teeth, hissed like a tiger – she didn't know what a tiger was, but her hiss would have made any tiger proud – and she let her body writhe like a barbed serpent, scratching at every piece of wood, twig, branch and leaf that came within reach of her sharp claws.

"Hey!" shrieked the Redwood, "Cut that out!"

Wunmor jumped loose and ran away, keeping close to the ground and rocks where the trees couldn't catch her.

Burnt and the pig watched Wunmor scurry away.

"She could've at least let us fill our jugs one more time before she took it," complained one of the unseelies. It didn't matter which one, as they had all been complaining most of the time since catching up with Edwina, and the goblin was growing tired of it.

"Yer a fairy," chided Edwina, "and that old witch don't like fairies. What'd you expect?"

"But I'm so thirsty!" wailed an unseelie.

"There's a creek somewhere over there." Edwina pointed in a general direction. "Go and get yourself some water."

"It's not the same!"

"And we see's you gots your bag o'eyes back, all nice and pretty," sneered an unseelie, pointing a long finger at the pouch hanging on Edwina's belt.

"Yeah?" said Edwina. "What of it?"

"You traded at our expense is what's of it," said the unseelie.

"It needed fixin'!" snapped the goblin. "And, besides, that weren't your goat anyways, so it's gots nothin' to do with you."

"What's so important about that stupid ol' bag anyway?" said the unseelie.

"That's none of yer biznezz," said Edwina.

"Oh, that poor, poor old goat," cried an unseelie from the back of the group.

"Probably all covered in cats by now," howled another.

Edwina shivered at the thought. "You lot needs to shut up, is what ya needs to do," she snapped. "I don't wanna hear no mores about cats or witches or goats. We's just gotta get that rotten Moggybairn, and then get to gettin' things fixed."

The unseelies glared at the goblin, and, huddling together, put some distance between themselves and Edwina. Not too much distance, as they didn't want to be separated, but enough that their peeving could continue without her intervening with halfway logical nonsense.

Occasionally, as she walked, Edwina would give a little hop to see over the tops of the grasses. She could smell the likhos, as well as several other breeds of goblin. *Could be good,* she thought, *could be not so good.* Sniffing the air again, squinting her eyes in concentration, her nostrils pinpointed the thin stream of Moggybairn scent, and she followed her crooked and excitedly fluttering proboscis.

According to her nose, the cat-baby was stationary. Up high. *Probably sitting in a tree,* she thought. She grew a bit concerned when her nose told her the thing was no longer in the tree. And then it told her there was something else familiar there. *The likho!* her mind said, not knowing Burnt's name. "And my piggy!" she declared aloud with glee. She looked behind her. Thankfully, the unseelies had neither heard nor seen her joy. *Gots to keep up appearances,* she thought, and she grumbled a bit, for good measure.

Twenty-Seven

*W*unmor scurried across the ground, jumping over roots and low-hanging vines. She decided, since she hadn't yet figured out how to determine whether a tree was a likho or not, it was best to avoid them all. Running past a mound of rocks, she noticed a hole underneath the pile that looked to be just big enough for her to fit. She dove into the earthen tunnel. When she felt she'd gone far enough she turned to look from where she'd come. After a bit, when it appeared nothing was coming after her, she thought it might be a good moment to rest her eyes and catch her breath.

She laid on her belly, her arms and legs tucked beneath, and lowered her chin to the ground. As she was just beginning to drift into a nice nap, she felt a tugging at her tail. She tried to pull the tail back up to curl it around herself, but she couldn't. The tugging continued. In front of her, she saw tracks in the dirt, left behind by her body as she was pulled backwards by whatever it was that was dragging her by the tail. Her claws came out and she tried to grasp at the ground, but the soil sifted between her toes and fingers.

The baby-half of her was too young to know the potential dangers of being dragged backwards into a hole under a mound of rocks in the middle of the Goblin Forest, so she wasn't frightened. She was curious.

The cat-half of her decided that, since at least part of her was cat, this must be exactly what she wanted and had intended all along.

Tug by tug, the trail in front of Wunmor grew longer and longer, until she was deep enough into the tunnel that she could no longer see the entrance. The slitted pupils in her eyes grew round, and she watched in reverse where she was being taken. There wasn't much to see. It was an earthen tunnel, fairly rounded on all sides, a few tendrils of roots hung down into it here and there, tickling her ears as she passed under them. The shift in weight towards her bottom let her know she was being pulled down a declining slope.

Her pointed ears turned and listened. She could hear whispers and grunts that coordinated with the tugs on her tail. Further behind those sounds, she heard chattering in what sounded like a small chamber. Her triangle nose found a scent that was both familiar and not, and her whiskers told her the air was clean. When one last and final tug pulled her into the chamber, she was delighted, not only because the tugging had stopped, but also because of the place she found herself to be.

The chamber was well-lit, with little fires in strategically-placed notches around the sides. It was large enough that Wunmor could stand up on her hind cat legs and pull herself to her full height. However, she chose to remain on her belly exactly where the dragging had stopped.

There were hundreds of fairies. Some stood in a circle on the ground around her. Some sat in seats carved into the walls of the chamber. Some hung from dangling roots. Each of them was thin, with long arms and legs that ended in large hands and feet. They had pointed noses, and their long hair was stringy, tangled and the color of dark bark. Tunics made of woven grass hung on their lanky bodies. Wunmor recognized the slightly familiar scent as being similar to the unseelies, but these fairies were a fraction of the size of those who'd accompanied her on the goat. And they were all, every single one of them, talking excitedly in voices that were also fractionally small.

Wunmor waited until her senses told her where each fairy was, then, slowly, she sat up. The chattering stopped. She turned her head in either direction, gazing at the people who gazed right back at her. She smiled. They smiled. And the chattering began again.

"I've never seen one like this b'fore," said one of the tiny voices.

"It's got ta be one of a kind," said another.

"There's human innit, but – "

"But also's some cat."

"I'm sensin' the Moggyfrau in this." This tiny voice sounded a bit nervous, but quickly recovered. "D'ya think it could be kin to the cat-lady."

"It's too big to be kin to the Moggyfrau. That witch is barely bigger'n us, and this thing's much larger."

Wunmor yawned.

"Oooeeee… lookit them teeth!" squealed a fairy.

"Whaddaya think we should do's with it?'

With this question, they all stopped and looked at Wunmor. One of them stepped forward.

"Beggin' yer pardon," it said, "but does ya have a name?"

Wunmor stared at the fairy for a moment, then giggled.

"It's just a baby," said another fairy. "And it looks ta be part human."

"As I recall," said yet another, "humans ain'tn't born talkin'."

"That's right. They needs ta learn it."

"Well, thats won't work for us. We needs ta help it along, I say."

One of the fairies raised its tiny voice and called out, "Are we all in agreement with that?"

Hundreds of tiny voices chattered, and then, suddenly, it was very quiet. There was a low hum, and the air grew thick. The hum grew louder, stronger, with the air keeping pace until Wunmor felt like her head was in a moist, overblown balloon. You might think it would be unpleasant, but it wasn't. It tickled and tingled and plucked at every hair on her head.

Louder and louder the humming filled the chamber, and filled the invisible balloon around Wunmor's head. And when it couldn't get any louder, when every hair on the Moggybairn's body was standing on their rooted tippy-toes...

LOCU! yelled hundreds of tiny voices at once, and hundreds of tiny pairs of oversized hands on skinny arms gave a single, resounding *CLAP!* and hundreds of tiny oversized bare feet *STOMPED!* once, in unison.

It was quiet again.

Wunmor gazed at the fairies.

The hundreds of fairies looked at the Moggybairn.

"That tickled!" Wunmor squealed, and she rolled on her back, kicking her legs in the air, laughing and laughing until she was all out of giggles. Then she rolled back onto her belly, and looked at the fairies standing around her. "Do it again!" she grinned, showing her sharp teeth behind the happy smile.

Twenty-Eight

"Sshhhh! We're getting' near," Edwina hissed over her shoulder to the loudly whispering unseelies behind her.

"How can you catch her smell over all them likhos?" hissed an unseelie back at her.

"They's distinctly diff'rent," Edwina snorted.

The fairies closed the distance between themselves and Edwina, not wanting there to be any uncertainty that they were with a goblin when entering a place called the Goblin Forest.

"Quit breathin' down me neck!" Edwina slapped a skinny arm behind her, brushing two unseelies off her back, only to have them jump back on, along with the other ten, and attach themselves to her as she stepped across the boundary from grass to forest. The goblin shook her entire body, flapping the unwanted passengers to the ground. The unseelies immediately got up and huddled as close as they could to her. Edwina considered chasing them off by releasing the gas that was building up within her, but she decided to save it. *You never know when a good belch or fart might come in handy when you're in the Goblin Forest,* she thought.

Trudging through the woods, Edwina once again found herself missing her pig. It was an agile thing, and traversing over the roots and vines would have been easy for the swine. She had to admit it would be nice if the magpie was with them, too. The bird was annoying as could be, but having it fly over the trees in search of the dratted cat-baby could save her some time. *Bah!* she thought. *Who needs 'em? I can do just fine by myself.* She tried to grin, but couldn't even muster a sneer. *My heart and my head ain't agreein', but no matter,* she told herself, and jumped over a large pile of rocks.

"Wait a minute!" whispered an unseelie.

"What?" said Edwina. Five unseelies, not seeing she'd stopped, bounced into and off of her rump. "Why?"

The twelve unseelies scanned the dirt and rocks, pointing at this and that, observing something that Edwina couldn't see.

"There's a buncha them," said an unseelie. "And they don't seem too concerned about leavin' a trail behind."

"Buncha what?" said Edwina, looking askance.

217

"That coulds mean a coupl'a things," said another unseelie. "They's either fierce or careless."

"What kind d'ya thinks they are?" said another unseelie, carefully inspecting a small stone.

"I doubt they's seelies. Them're too lah-dee-dah to be found inna goblin's forest."

"Not to mention they's gone underground," said another unseelie.

"What?" Edwina yipped.

"Fairies," said an unseelie.

"Unseelies-ish like us," said another unseelie who was a bit more excited than the first.

"Maybe, but we's can't be too sure until we sees 'em."

The unseelie who'd been inspecting the stone, followed it to another stone, then another, then stood and pointed at a hole in the ground. "They're in there." It stood up and pointed, unnecessarily.

Edwina pressed her nose to the hole in the ground and took a deep draft. "I don't know what kind've whatnots you's're talkin' about, but what I *do* knows is that the Moggybairn's in there with em."

Without hesitation, the unseelies climbed into the hole and made their way down the tunnel. Although the tops of their heads touched the earthen ceiling, they were able to walk fairly easily if they hunched over just a bit. Edwina, however, found herself crawling on her bony hands and knees, with her ears tied above her head so as not to squish them under her knees. It was the perfect opportunity for some good and heartfelt grumbling, and she made use of the time by doing just that. She didn't particularly like the unseelies, at least not any more than anything else in the world, and the idea of meeting more of them wasn't on her list, albeit a very short list, of enjoyable things to do. '*Untrustworthy little nits*' was one of the things she grumbled, along with her personal feelings about their smell, how they dressed, what they looked like, how they talked, and what she assumed they ate. But she kept crawling. Partly because the tunnel was too narrow to turn around, but mostly because the aroma of the infant grew stronger the further she crawled.

When they finally reached the chamber, Edwina was relieved to be able to sit properly and untie her ears. She checked to make sure the pouch full of eyes was still on her belt, and she rested her hand on the bag so ensure no '*sneekin' little thievin' fairy*' could snatch it away. She squinted her eyes and gave a warning look to the entire room. Nobody noticed. If they *had* noticed, nobody would have cared.

As for the unseelies, it was as if they'd met distant cousins for the first time, which was more or less what they had done. One of them turned to Edwina and smiled.

"These're our distant cousins," it said. "We've heard tell of 'em, but hadn't yet met each-uthers." Big hands on its narrow hips, it sighed, "Too bad we don't got none of that old goat's milk. If ever there was a time for celebratin' this would be one of 'em."

"They's unseelies?" said Edwina. "Why's they so small?"

"Not unseelies," the unseelie said. "Aoseelies. Unseelies live in the grasses. Aoseelies live under the ground in the woods."

"Is that why they's a fraction of yer size?" Edwina looked over her shoulder, checking to be sure none had snuck up behind her.

"Prob'ly. But otherwise they're mostly just like us."

Edwina looked around at the throng of fairies. To her eyes the small ones looked just the same as the large. Tunics and long, tangled hair. Oversized feet and hands at the ends of long and skinny arms and legs.

"Mostly?" Edwina raised a kinked eyebrow.

"Well, they's gots a bit o'magic in 'em."

"Like that seelie at the pond?"

The unseelie gasped, stepped back and sneered, pointing a long finger at the hobgoblin, "You watch what you say, goblin. Them seelies ain't *nothin'* like us. You's best not to be makin' no comparisons."

Edwina gave a "*humph!*" and tucked away a note in her mind that she'd discovered a way to insult the scrawny pests. Then she looked to the Moggybairn. "I s'pose that's how the thing's talkin' now?"

The unseelie turned and resumed its happy composure. "Yep. They's done the *locu* on her."

"What's that mean?"

"Means she can talk."

"She learnt it all at once?"

"Humans is the only creatures that can't talk when they enter the world," said the unseelie. "Them aoseelies just pulled on the cat part that's in her, and plumped up the ability." It stood akimbo and proud, as if it was the unseelies themselves who'd performed the act. "The talkin' came easy to her, and app'rntly she's been watchin' everything." It looked at the goblin. "She knows everything's that's happened," it said, "includin' you stealin' her and thinkin' about havin' her for dinner."

"She heard that, huh?" said the goblin, tucking away another note in her mind to be careful around the Moggybairn. Which prompted a question. "Does she got a name?"

"Yep, she tells us it's — "

"Yeeessss?" Edwina rubbed her bony hands together in anticipation.

"Hah! Nice try," laughed the unseelie. "Ain'tn't no ways I'm'a tellin' you her name."

Edwina scowled and muttered a few colorfully descriptive words for her feelings about that.

A small group of aoseelies approached the unseelie and the goblin. Edwina wrapped her fingers tighter around the pouch on her belt. She wasn't sure how or why she knew they were thieves, and it didn't matter how much truth there was to the idea. She just knew they were.

"That Wu — " started one of the aoseelies.

Edwina's ears twitched.

"Shush!" said the unseelie. "Don't forget we's gots a goblin in our midst."

Edwina grumbled and pretended to pick something from between her toes.

"That baby's got some tales," said the aoseelies. "Seems she's been witness to a league of likhos, one of whom's been doin' curses on her brudders."

Edwina smiled. *Hah!* she thought. *I was right!*

"And," the aoseelie continued, "a curse on somethin' you's mights be havin' on ya." It nodded towards the bag on the hobgoblin's belt.

Edwina's smile disappeared. "Nope," she said. "'Twas only upon them humans."

"Not accordin' to the likhos."

"How's can she know fer sure?" asked Edwina. "Only them's that was there at the time would know." *And I was one of 'em and even I'm's not steady upon it,* she thought.

"One of them likhos in the league was the one that done the cursin'."

Edwina squinted her eyes, groused inarticulately under her breath, and clutched her bag of eyes with both hands. *That would explain a lot,* she thought.

While the likhos lumbered about, trying to give chase to the quick-footed Moggybairn, Burnt backed away into the trees surrounding them. The teasing and cajoling had become tiresome, and having to answer to any of them was more than it cared to continue doing.

Once sure the others wouldn't see, Burnt stood, straightening its trunk and wriggling life back into its roots. It watched its arboreal cousins tripping over themselves, and let a small chuckle slip past its wooden lips. They'd laughed when Burnt had chosen to leave the Goblin Forest to live amongst things that were not likhos, and they relished every error and mishap the emigrant tree had encountered. But what they didn't realize was all that Burnt had accomplished. Dinners and curses might not have turned out as planned, but the wandering goblin-tree had learned about the creatures that lived beyond the Goblin Forest, and there were many different creatures to be learnt about. Most useful, Burnt had found, was that each had their own peculiar scent. Secluded to the center of the forest, most goblin-trees could tell if something was goblin, fairy, or something that might be good in a stew. Burnt, however, knew *which* goblin, *which* fairies, and *which* stew options they were. And now… letting its leaves sift through the scents floating in the air… Burnt recognized her.

'Edwina!' Burnt thought. *'I should have known she'd be following that Moggybairn.'* The likho's leaves rustled. *'And she's got the unseelies with her.'*

The rustling shifted, and a new aroma reached the likho's leaves. Burnt looked to the full moon in the sky. "Not long until it sets," it said, bending to pick up the pink pig nibbling at the sprouts of turf at its feet. "We need to move quickly."

The likhos, having given up chasing Wunmor, sat back down by the fire, ready to resume the verbal skewering of Burnt.

"Where'd that burned up excuse for a likho go?" asked the Redwood.

Twenty-Nine

*D*issun, Dudderun and Aldbrecht chatted the evening away – rather, Dissun and Dudderun mostly chattered and Aldbrecht mostly listened – and by the time the twins fell asleep the vulfusgrump knew about the unseelies and their fondness for the milk of an old goat, that a bunch of old hobgoblin hags weren't blind anymore because now they had frog eyes, that a likho had tried to eat them, and that there was a goblin named Edwina who was bent on having their baby sister for dinner. Oh, and their mum wasn't very happy with them at the moment.

As the boys slumbered, the vulfusgrump looked through the window, watching the moon set. When the first tentacles of morning sun crept through the seams around the door Aldbrecht was waiting at the door. No longer a cranky old man – at least until the full moon rose again that night – he stood on four legs with heavy paws. A thick coat of gray covered his wolf body from his head to the tip of his tail. The overalls he'd worn the day before hung on a hook by the door. Dissun and Dudderun wiped the sleep from their eyes and, after adjusting to the sight of the wolf, they looked at the empty basket on the hearth, wishing they'd saved a bit for breakfast.

From their lopsided conversation the night before, they knew Aldbrecht lived on the other side of the Goblin Forest, and that he came to this brick house during the full moon. They didn't know much else.

"How'd you find this house to stay in?" asked Dudderun as they passed through the door on their way out. "Wasn't you concerned the owner might come back?"

"It had been abandoned for quite a while when I found it." Aldbrecht nosed the door shut, stood on his hind legs and set the latch in place with a padded toe. "And from what was left behind you'd think a family of swine had lived here."

"All the pigs we known of's been fairly clean creatures," said Dissun.

"There was a dried up mud bath in the middle of the room," said the wolf.

"Well, they's do like their mud," said Dudderun. "Otherwise, pigs bein' unclean is one of them old wives tales."

"Speakin' of which," said Dissun, turning to the wolf, "do you by any chance know whether that means the tale is old or the wives?"

Aldbrecht paused to look at the boys. "Probably both," he said, and padded down the steps.

The league of likhos were so busy trying find Burnt they didn't see the blackened tree tiptoeing in a wide circle around them, the pink pig riding atop its head.

Burnt's leaves gently sniffed the air, rustling in the direction they should go if they wanted to find the hobgoblin Edwina. Once clear of the others, Burnt lengthened his stride and quickly traversed across the forest. By the time the moon was setting, the goblin-tree and its pink passenger were very close to where Edwina's odor blanketed the forest floor.

Atop the jagged head of the likho, the pink pig squealed and stamped its hooves in excitement.

"Hold on a minute," said Burnt, reaching up to extract the pig from its perch. It set the swine on the ground. "There you go. You happy now?"

The pig danced in circles, making sharp yipping sounds, then turned and ran ahead of the tree, grunting with each cloven bounce.

The Moggyfrau, on her broom with thirteen cats, flew through the mist rising from the grass. The thin fog veiled her approach, and when she reached the boundary between the forest and field, she was comfortable in the knowledge that nobody had seen her. She descended, disembarking once her feet touched the ground. Flying over hills and fields was fine, but trying to fly between the trees of a forest could be treacherous – and if that forest was a Goblin Forest… the Moggyfrau chose not to consider what might happen if she were to attempt such foolishness.

It didn't take long for the horde of cats to catch up, and soon the field's tall switchgrass was rustling with more felines than a mouse could dream of in its worst nightmare.

Grasping the shaft of the broom in one fist, balancing it in her hand so the whisk wouldn't drag in the dirt, the Moggyfrau crossed the boundary and made her way into the forest. She didn't look back. There was no need. She knew each and every cat was with her. She walked with purpose, determinedly striding over – never upon – the twigs debris that made up the ground-floor of the forest. The sleek black cat who'd sat at the fore of her broom walked beside her.

"Mind that you don't step on any of them leaves or twigs," the Moggyfrau said to the cat. "You never know what might be hidin' within them things."

The cat nodded. It already knew this.

"Just keep on goin' down this path," continued the Moggyfrau. "My skin's a'tinglin' with the hue of magic floatin' across from over thataway."

The cat nodded. It already knew this, as well.

"And keep a wary eye," said the Moggyfrau, "every bump could be home to a hogboon. The last thing we wants is them varmints crawlin' up our whatnots."

The cat sighed. "Hogboons. Leprechauns. Kobolds… I know what's in the Goblin Forest. It's why it's called the Goblin Forest." The cat wanted to suggest the Moggyfrau hush herself, but, even though it was a cat and therefore fettered by none, she was a witch and it was generally better not to make such suggestions to witches – even tiny ones.

The Moggyfrau considered suggesting to the cat that it mind its tone, but instead she bobbed her dandelion head from side to side silently mouthing a few choice words.

"I heard that," said the cat.

"Good," said the Moggyfrau.

"Aoseelies, pixies, gnomes…" the cat sniffed the air, "and a family of badgers."

"Badgers, you say?"

The cat twitched the whiskers. "Just ahead of us, and a bit off the path."

"Hmmm…. off the path makes sense. That's what I'd do if I was a badger. And what about the others? Where's they?"

"Hard to tell with the gnomes, they smell so much like the woods they live in, and they move around a lot. Aoseelies are up ahead, in the direction we're going. Pixies," the cat ruffled the hair up and down its spine, "are everywhere."

"Like fleas, them pixies are. No matter. They're harmless."

"They're annoying."

"True, but they won't hurt nothin'. Not by much, anyway. Just don't let 'em get betwixt your toes."

The cat nodded. It already knew this, too, but it put a bit more ginger in its step nonetheless.

"I'm more interested in whatever it that I'm not sensin'."

"Perhaps it's aoseelies. You know they're able to hide within their magic."

The Moggyfrau had heard of fairies with magic that could keep them unseen to witches. She felt such skills were cowhearted, and she assured herself that abilities like those would be wasted upon her as she would never be tempted to use them. On top of all that, she felt a little bit jealous.

"Don't sulk," said the cat.

"I'm not sulking."

"It's unbecoming of a witch."

"I *said* I'm not sulking!"

The cat snorted but left it at that.

Thirty

*T*he magpie stood at the entrance of Edwina's cave, watching the sun rise. It had tried to sleep, but couldn't. Not even when it pulled a few extra nuggets of silver and gold into the nest.

"That was one of the longest nights I've ever seen," it grumbled. It stretched one skinny leg, then the next, turned its neck to both sides, and ruffled the feathers along its back down to the tip of its tail – and it launched itself upwards. The bird tilted this way and that along the breeze, and when it spied what it was looking for it flapped its wings and flew in the direction of the Goblin Forest.

Edwina's knobby back ached from laying all night in the odd-shaped hole at the side of the aoseelies' underground home. She'd tried to sleep but the reveling of the fairies had kept her awake most of the night. The goblin rolled out of her makeshift earthen bed and stood up. All around her, unseelies and aoeseelies slept soundly in small piles. Even the pops and cracks of the hobgoblin's distorted bones and joints when she stretched out her arms and legs didn't wake them. Edwina considered kicking and knocking over a few of the piles, partly for fun and partly for payback for her own lack of sleep. *Eh,* she thought, *that'll just wake 'em up,* and she carefully stepped over and tiptoed around them instead. She was watching her big feet so much, she almost didn't see Wunmor crawling out of the chamber and disappearing into the tunnel.

"Oh, ho!" Edwina snapped. "No you don't!" She leapt across the room and ran after the Moggybairn.

Wunmor giggled as she made her way through the tunnel.

Edwina crawled after her. She'd rushed so fast she didn't have time to tie up her ears and she cursed each time she knelt on a floppy lobe.

The tunnel was long, and Edwina was suspecting it had grown longer overnight. It curved and twisted and turned, allowing glimpses of the baby ahead of her but never letting her get close enough to reach out and catch it. Her shriveled heart bumped a slightly larger beat when she saw the first shaft of light indicating she was nearing the outside world, and just as she rounded the last turn she saw Wunmor's feet bounding away. The goblin scrambled the last stretch of tunnel and tumbled out through the hole in the rocks. She jumped to her feet, looking every which way, then upwards when she heard giggling coming from the treetops.

"Get down here!" Edwina screeched at the Moggybairn.

"No!" said Wunmor. She stuck her tongue out gave the goblin a very wet raspberry.

Edwina straightened herself, as much as she could with a goblin's body, cleared her throat and, with the sweetest voice she could muster, said, "If you come down here we can have some breakfast together."

"No!" said Wunmor, and she dashed along the branch on which she'd been sitting, all the way out to the tip, and jumped to the next branch. Then the next, and the next.

Edwina ran, one eye on the Moggybairn, the other on the roots of trees that moved and jumped in front of her. She vaulted over some, crawled under others. *So close,* she thought, *can't let her get away again!*

Moments after the goblin had left the tunnel, the pink pig emerged from the trees, followed by Burnt. The pig scampered to the pile of rocks and stuck its nose in the hole. It sniffed. It sniffed again. It oinked and sniffed some more. It withdrew its snout and sniffed the ground. With a surprised squeal, it looked up and ran after the scent of its goblin.

Burnt waited a moment. The likho didn't particularly like the idea of going back into the forest where they might run into the league again. But abandoning the pig to the Goblin Forest wasn't something it wanted on its conscience. It heaved a sigh and followed at an unenthusiastic pace.

"I don't think we'd've seen this path if it weren't for you," said Dudderun.

"That is the intention." Aldbrecht paused for a moment, sniffed a shrub, then continued.

"We surely do appreciate you helpin' us to find our baby sister," said Dissun. It was the eleventh time he or his brother had expressed their appreciation to the wolf.

"As I said ten times before, don't mention it."

They walked a bit further, and the forest grew thicker as they went.

"I'm not sure if'n I'm likin' this," said Dudderun. "It don't feel natural."

"We *are* in the Goblin Forest," Aldbrecht said. "I suppose you could say that unnatural is natural here."

"Why do they call it the Goblin Forest?" Dissun looked around, gesturing to make his point. "It don't look no diff'rnt from any other forest we've seen."

"Because the goblins wanted to call it that and nobody felt like arguing with them about it."

"I guess that makes sense," said Dissun. "From the few goblins we've met we've found there ain't no talkin' rightly with any of 'em."

After a bit more walking, Dudderun cleared his throat. "A thought just occurred to me," he said.

"What're ya thinkin'?" said Dissun.

"I can hardly wait to hear it," said Aldbrecht.

"I'm hopin' you'll excuse me if this is an impolite question...," said Dudderun.

"Yes?" said the wolf.

"How is it that you can talk human? I mean, it made sense last night when you *was* a human —"

"I *wasn't* human. I only *looked* like one."

"But," Dudderun continued unabashed, "it made sense that you could talk human last night. But now that yer in yer wolf form, why ain't you just, I dunno, talkin' like a wolf?"

"It's a side effect of being a vulfusgrump. During the three days of the full moon I can speak both my own and the human languages. Tonight is the third night. After that I'll be back to speaking only wolf. And it will be a great relief."

"Why's that?" asked Dissun.

"Because then it will be easier to ignore you," said Albrecht.

The wolf stopped, perking his ears and angling them in directions.

"What?" asked Dudderun.

"Hush," said the wolf. He sniffed the air, "This is unusual..."

"That don't sound comforting." Dissun tried to see what the wolf was sniffing.

The wolf breathed in deeply, then snorted the air out. "Something's afoot."

"Afoot?"

"Whose foot?"

"Afoot," snarled the wolf. "Afoot. Something's happening." He jutted his nose toward the depth of the forest. "Over there."

"You think it might be our sister?" asked Dudderun.

"Could be. The smell is... off."

"Then we gotsta go thataway." Dissun turned off the path, and his brother followed him.

"I don't," said Aldbrecht.

Dudderun turned to the wolf. "But...!" His eyes darted in all directions. "We's gonna get eaten if we's by ourselves."

"Why do you think that?" asked the wolf.

"Because that's what happens in the woods. Things're all about tryin' to eats ya."

The wolf cocked one ear. "Who told you that?"

"Our mum," said Dissun.

"Your mother," said the wolf. "Do you think, by chance, she might just have been trying to keep you fools from going into the woods?"

The boys looked at each other, then back at the wolf.

"I've already told you, several times, you two are not tempting to the palate," said the wolf. "You have an aroma that offends the olfactories and would likely cause even the most hardened taste-bud to cringe. You'd be too chewy. And there's a curse hanging over your heads."

"Well," Dudderun said after a bit of thinking, "that just makes it all that much more okay fer us to go thataway. We gotsta get our sister."

"That, or we just head on down the road never to return home," added Dissun.

"But," said Dudderun, looking at his brother, "I'm comin' to think that maybe we's should be gettin' our sister just because she's our sister."

"Yeah," agreed Dissun, "I s'pose you're right, what with her bein' family and all."

They turned to Aldbrecht. "So, you comin' or not?"

The wolf looked at the boys, turned his head to look homewards, then turned back to the boys and stepped off the path to join them. "I could always use a good story to tell the pack upon my return."

Thirty-One

*T*he magpie circled above the Goblin Forest.

"Woot!" it said to itself as it looked down and saw the goblin. "There she is."

The bird tilted its head low, readying to dive down and swoop in upon its mark. It snapped its head back up when it saw more movement than Edwina should be making.

"What is that thing?" it said when it saw the Moggybairn hopping from branch to branch.

The black-beaded eyes on either side of the bird's head flicked back and forth.

It saw the likho following a pink pig. This made the bird smile a little. It liked the pig and was glad to see the little swine was okay.

It caught view of two boys and a wolf. *Not them!* thought the bird, and its smile wavered.

Then it saw the little witch, dressed in black, dandelion head bobbing as she walked, carrying a broom, with a horde of cats following her. The bird's smile disappeared.

In the middle of it all, a league of likhos were milling about, pixies were flitting everywhere, hogboons were gathering in the neatly mowed front lawn of a red brick house, and a large number of fairies were flooding out from a hole in a pile of rocks and washing across the forest floor. The magpie recognized the unseelies, but not the other fairies.

Using its corvid instincts, the black bird tracked the paths of everything it saw and judged that, excepting the hogboons, they all seemed to be going in the direction where they would soon converge upon each other.

"This doesn't look good," said the magpie.

Something should probably be done about it, said one voice in the bird's head.

But not necessarily by me, said another voice.

The pig's down there.

Oh, all right!

The magpie tilted one wing and turned towards the place where the humans kept their farm.

❖

Wunmor hopped from tree to tree with the goblin chasing her from below.

"Stop yer runnin'," Edwina yelled after the Moggybairn. "I only's wants to have ya for breakfast." She panted and rephrased, "I means to have breakfast *with* ya! I ain'tn't gonna eats ya." She ran some more, keeping her attention on the baby running in the trees with such intent she almost didn't notice the shift in the air that made the hairs on her back stand up. *What's that?* she thought, and looked over her shoulder. *No! Not her. Not when I'm so close!* The hobgoblin bent forward and ran raster.

Branches grabbed at Wunmor as she ran. She didn't know what cursing was, but she heard what she recognized as a great deal of unfriendliness each time she slipped through their twiggy fingers. She made a point to dig her claws in deeper, just to see if that increased the cursing. It did.

Trees sound funny when they're mad, thought Wunmor. She flicked her cat tail and darted between two limbs that were trying to grab her between their leafy fists. Another sound came to her, a new one to her pointed ears yet somehow familiar. It sounded like the noises she heard when she dreamed. There it was again! Neither slowing nor missing a step, she looked aside and saw a creature that looked like her. That is, it looked like the back half of her.

"Hello," said the orange tabby on the tree next to Wunmor. It easily jumped from branch to branch, keeping pace with her.

"Who are you?" Wunmor hopped to another tree.

"I'm – " The tabby made a strange sound which was its name in the language of cats. "I'm with the Moggyfrau."

"What's a Moggyfrau?"

"She's a witch."

Wunmor wasn't sure what that was, but had a feeling it had something to do with her.

"Look down," said the tabby.

Wunmor looked down and saw cats running below. She couldn't count, but there were a lot of them. In the midst of the multitude of felines was Edwina. The goblin didn't look happy.

"That's the Moggyfrau, coming up behind the horde," said the orange cat.

Behind the mob of cats Wunmor saw a very small woman with a head that looked like a dandelion. Alongside the woman walked a sleek, black cat. The pair appeared to be walking at an unhurried step, yet somehow they were keeping up with the cats running before them.

"She's tiny," said Wunmor.

"Only on the outside," said the cat.

Dissun and Dudderun half followed, half led the way that took them deeper into the forest.

"You says we're not in danger of bein' eaten," said Dudderun, "but what with this bein' a Goblin Forest I'm bettin' there's other things we should be watchin' for."

Dissun nodded in agreement. "A bit of knowin' upon that might be a way to pass the time, if nothin' else."

"Well," the wolf hopped over a fallen log, "do you remember the hogboons I told you about?"

"Them's the ones that brings you food, right?"

"Yes. They live under mounds on the forest floor, so you should be careful where you step."

Both boys purposed their eyes to watch for mounds.

"What happens if you steps on one of 'em?"

"Besides ruining their home?" said Aldbrecht.

"Yeah, besides that."

"They're quick little creatures and they'll climb all over you, getting into your shirt and shoes. They'd do that anyway to any passerby, but if you've ruined their home they'll be angry. They don't really hurt you, but they can be very annoying."

"We don't got shoes," said Dissun, looking down at his dirty, bare feet.

"Which brings us to the pixies," said the wolf. "They're tiny. So small you can't see them. If you step amongst them they can get stuck between your toes."

"And then what?"

"They have very sharp teeth." They walked a few paces. "I haven't seen an ogre in here for some time, but you can be certain they here. And the trowes…" the wolf shuddered and shook its fur. "You definitely do not want to lay eyes upon one of those."

"Why not?"

"They're quite ugly."

"We've seen ugly things," Dudderun said confidently.

"Not like this," said the wolf. "If you see one of them you'll never want to open your eyes again. Ever." He thought for a moment, then said, "The biggest nuisance you're most likely going to encounter are the goblin-trees. The likhos."

"We's almost got eaten up by one of those!" said Dissun.

"Yes, you told me that last night," said Aldbrecht. "But that was only one. In the Goblin Forest they gather in leagues."

"A league of trees that're goblins…," Dudderun pondered aloud.

"It's not as fun as it sounds," said the wolf, then he stopped short. "Hold your step," he said. "Do you hear that?"

The boys narrowed their ears and listened intently.

Coming from deeper into the forest came a familiar sound.

"Them's cats!" said Dudderun.

"The Moggyfrau!" said Dissun.

Without another word, the two boys darted off in the direction of the mewling cats.

"Wait a minute!" Aldbrecht ran behind them. "You can't just go running into the middle of the forest without knowing what's going on."

Dissun and Dudderun ignored the wolf's advice, kicking up their speed a bit instead. They ran over rocks, dodging whatever looked like a mound. They splashed across a small stream, calling apologies over their shoulders to the gnome with a fishing rod. The more they ran the louder the caterwauling got, spurring them onward.

Aldbrecht followed at a lope, curious and amused. Then he felt the drift of something in the air. An old, very old, familiar scent. "Stop!" he barked at the boys. But they kept running. "Drat!" He caught up to the boys, ran in front of them and stopped, causing them to tumble over him. "Stop," he said. "There's more ahead than your sister and some cats."

Dissun, bending at the hips with his hands on his knees, worked to catch his breath. Dudderun stood upright, panting as much as his brother.

Aldbrecht nodded his nose, pointing towards a thicket. "Just beyond those shrubs. She's there. At least, I'm pretty sure it would be your sister. The scent is similar. And there is the distinct aroma of cats. But that's not all…" The wolf peered ahead, all of his senses focused on what lay shortly beyond. "I smell a hobgoblin."

"Edwina!" said Dissun.

"And fairies…"

"The Unseelies," smiled Dudderun.

"Two different kinds of fairies."

The boys looked at each other.

"We's only knows the Unseelies," said Dissun.

"Several likhos, one of them smells of burnt wood."

"That'd be the one that tried to have us for dinner," said Dudderun.

"...and...," the wolf looked aside at the boys, "...a pig?"

"Oh, the pig's a pal with that Edwina hobgoblin," said Dissun. "It's a nice little thing."

Thirty-Two

*T*he clearing in the midst of the forest was quiet and still. A few of the more daring birds flitted down to see if there might be any chokeberries or acorns lying about. Most of the birds, however, kept themselves at a safe distance. They knew that at any moment the calm and tranquility could be shattered.

And they were right.

"Why'd you let her get away?" shouted the Redwood. It was yelling at the trees and shrub that were walking close behind.

"Nobody *let* her get away," said the Pine.

"If I remember right," the Chokeberry rustled past everyone and into the clearing, "it was you who dropped her."

"Yeah," said the Pine. "She gave you a little scratch and *whoop!* there she goes, right through your twiggy fingers."

"It wasn't a little scratch," said the Redwood, raising an arm-branch to look at its bark. "That's going to leave a scar."

"Oh…," the Willow cried, "I *wish* we could have a fire."

"We're trees," said the Oak. "It'd be a bit cannibalistic to build a fire, wouldn't you think?"

"But we're not *real* trees," wailed the Willow.

The league of likhos, grousing and complaining and accusing, were so focused on being livid with one another they didn't hear the snapping limbs and swishing of leaves growing steadily louder. But when they heard the angry roar of cats they stopped and looked to see where it was coming from.

If the likhos had shattered the tranquility of the clearing, what came now pulverized it and sent it to the winds.

Wunmor, leapt from a tree and landed at the top of the Oak, then an orange tabby jumped and landed on the Pine. The trees' uppermost branches swayed with the unexpected weight, and the Moggybairn and the cat dug their claws into the wood, gaining purchase and balance.

Hissing, meowing, snarling, and spatting, the horde of cats of every color, every size, and everything between fluffy and sleek, roared into what could now be described more as an arena than a clearing. In the midst of them was an extremely unhappy hobgoblin, and right behind her was a tiny witch.

Covering every inch of space left free came a flood of fairies. unseelies and aoseelies, piling over and on top of each other, climbing to see where the Moggybairn had gone. "There she is!" yelled one of them, and like a singular wave they washed up the trunk of the Oak to protectively surround Wunmor.

"Told you it was them," said the sleek black cat to the Moggyfrau.

The witch crossed her arms, with a *hmph!*

There was a pause. A very long, very intense series of moments, where everyone looked at each other, their eyes daring that someone make a move.

And then, with as much of a crash as a small swine could make, the pig jumped through the low-lying bramble and trotted into the center of the crowded clearing, followed by Burnt who chose to remain on the outskirts of the circle.

The pig squealed happily and ran to Edwina.

And everyone started arguing.

"They's sure do make a ruckus," whispered Dissun to his brother as he peered over the edge of the moss-covered log.

"You got that right," answered Dudderun, also whispering, "It is a fracas, but I fer sure can't make out none of what they's sayin'."

"Can pretty much get the gist of it all, though," said Dissun, still whispering. "They's all angry about some sorta stuff."

Aldbrecht, having just caught up to the boys, sauntered to where they were hiding behind the log. "There's no need to whisper," he said. "Nothing's going to hear you over all that commotion."

"So," said Dissun, although not whispering he still kept his voice low. "Whadda'y'all think we oughts to do?"

"You said you need to get your sister back," said Aldbrecht.

"Yeah?" said Dudderun.

"Then I suggest that's what you should do."

"Go into the midst of all that?" said Dudderun, his voice squeaking in its effort to remain low whilst expressing alarm.

"Perhaps not directly..." said the wolf.

"Lookit them Unseelies," Dissun pointed in the general direction of the green-haired fairies. "They's an ungrateful lot, they are."

"What're them other ones that look like 'em buts tinier?" Dudderun squinted his eyes to get a better look.

"Ah," said Aldbrecht. "Those would be the aoseelies."

"Who're they?"

"Kin of some sort to the unseelies," said the wolf. "Be careful around them. They've been known to cast a spell or two."

"Well, we don't need no more spells, that's for sure," said Dissun. "But we do needs to get our sister."

The two boys watched and pondered what they saw. They needed a plan, and good one at that. One that would get them what they wanted, while having a bit of fun with the goblins and fairies at the same time. Dissun looked around for frogs or worms or anything that might help. Dudderun rubbed his scalp, looked between his toes and stuffed his hands in his pockets. At the bottom of one of those pockets he felt something and pulled out a handful of cat hair.

"Lookit what I got," Didderun said to his brother.

Dissun dug into his pocket and retrieved his own handful of cat hair. Aldbrecht adverted his eyes as the grins spread across the boys' faces. They stuffed the hair back into their pockets and nodded.

"You comin' with us?" Dissun said to Aldbrecht.

"I wouldn't miss this for the world," said the wolf.

Thirty-Three

"Woot! Woot!" chittered the magpie, perched in a high branch of the tree that grew outside the house where the woman lived. "Woot! Woot!"

A half-chewed spud flew through the window, easily missing the bird.

The magpie stepped aside. "Woot! Woot!"

The door flew open and the woman stepped out onto the porch. She raised a fist in the air and began the first sounds of a curse, then, abruptly, stopped.

"It's a corvid," she called back to someone inside the house.

"A what?" came an old man's voice back at her.

"A corvid," she repeated. "A magpie."

"Hide the spoons and forks!" the old man shouted. "They's improper thiefs, they are."

The magpie ruffled its feathers, ignoring the suggestion that it was an improper thief. It *was* a thief, but not an *improper* one.

"Hush!" scolded the woman. "You don't want to be insulting it."

You got that right, thought the bird. Then it said, "Woot! Woot! Woot!" and shook its feathered head, turned and flew to the barn's loft. Momentarily, it came out with a sock in the talons of one foot. Birds don't have a sense of smell, but any bird, especially a corvid, knows you don't put the sock of a ten-year-old boy in your mouth. It flitted back down to the tree, dropping the sock at the woman's feet. When it was once again perched it shook its foot and wiped its toes clean on the branch. "Woot! Woot!" it said.

"I think it's trying to tell us something."

"Yeah," yelled the old man, "that it wants our silverware." He cackled. "Too bad we ain't got none." He raised his voice. "All's we gots is wooden spoons, ya stupid bird!" The old man cackled some more.

"Don't insult it," said the woman. When she had been a child she'd seen her own mother talking to black birds. Her grandmother, too. Most birds weren't helpful. Some were pretty, some were good to eat, but most kept what few thoughts they had to themselves and didn't pay much more attention to the humans than whether there was seed in the feeder. But corvids – black birds, crows, magpies, ravens – those birds were different. You had to show them respect. They were smart. The corvid could be tricky. It was often a thief. And, if you listened closely, it could tell you things.

"I'm sorry for what he says," the woman said to the bird. "He's just a senile old man." She said the last part louder and towards the inside of the house.

"Hah!" the old man retorted, but after that he was quiet.

She turned to the bird. "Oh, I wish I knew what you were saying," said the woman.

Ridiculous humans, the bird thought. *You knew well enough what I was saying ten years ago.* It cleared its throat, warbled a bit, then tried again.

"Can you understand me now?" the bird said.

"Yes. Now I know what you're saying," said the woman.

"Had to find my human dialect," said the magpie. "It's been ten years since I've cared to converse with a human. No offense."

"None taken," said the woman, and she went straight to the point. "What have my boys gotten into this time?"

"Those two boys of yours – " it stopped itself, remembering its manners, then began again. "I can't tell you what they've done because I don't know and I'd prefer not to imagine it. But, judging by what I've seen, they might be needing some of your help."

"By any chance is there a baby with them?"

"I can't tell you that either. Woot! Woot! But we need to go now!" it cawed. It flew out of the tree, away from the farm, back to the tree, repeating this several times.

"I'll follow you," said the woman.

"Not a bad idea!" The bird perched on a low branch of the tree, ruffling its feathers.

"Grandpa," the woman yelled into the house, "put your shoes on." She nodded to the magpie. "Just let me gather a few things."

It was shortly afterwards that the woman left the farm. She rode in a small wagon, driving a plump donkey that trotted as quickly as she could make it go. Grandpa sat in the bed of the cart, chewing on a spud. He held a small bag with more potatoes on his lap. Also in the wagon were a bag of chalk, a plank of wood shingle, and a plain wooden box held shut with a strap of old leather. The magpie stood on the donkey's head between its ears, pointing the way.

The path along the edge of the pond was fairly even and traversable in the wagon. It got a bit rough as it went past low hills and large rocks. When they got to the fields you couldn't see the path beneath the grasses, but no wheels got caught in a rut or came undone going over an oversized stone, and the woman kept the donkey moving. The donkey didn't mind this part of the journey so much, as quick snacks were within easy reach, and it chewed and chomped as it plodded along.

"Hold up now." The woman pulled on the reins and the donkey stopped.

"Why'd we stop?" said the old man, not bothering to turn around to look and see for himself.

"We're at the forest's edge," said the woman. "There's a distinct boundary betwixt it and the grass."

The donkey stared into the forest, into the thickness where the sun couldn't reach. It laid back its ears flat along its neck and brayed a series of honking, howling haws that made the grass around its hooves shake.

"Woot!" cawed the magpie, jumping off the donkey's head and flitting over to rest on a siderail of the wagon.

"Hush that thing up," said the old man. "It's gonna attract varmints and critters we don't wanna be meetin'!"

Not sure whether the man was talking about the donkey or itself, the magpie clicked its beak a few times, then kept it shut.

The woman hopped down from her seat and went to the donkey. "We've got to keep going," she said.

The donkey stopped its braying protestations, but refused to look the woman in the eye. It stomped one foot, digging its small hoof into the dirt as if anchoring itself.

"You stubborn little beast," the woman gently scolded the donkey. It was best to be considerate to the feelings of animals, especially those in a position of working for you. They could easily be of the mind to quit their job, especially if they were a donkey. She thought for a moment, then smiled. Pulling one long ear towards her mouth, she whispered into it. The donkey, it's ears standing at attention upon hearing the words she spoke, nodded, and the woman went back to the wagon and climbed up into the seat. She'd barely picked up the reins when the cart started moving, rolling onwards into the forest.

"What'd you say to it?" asked the old man.

"I told it that if it didn't want to continue it could stay behind with you."

The old man grumbled something the woman couldn't quite make out, and wouldn't have cared if she could.

As they rolled along, the path widened and narrowed, and made so many turns it wasn't clear which way they were headed.

"Is you sure we're still goin' in the right direction?" grumped the old man.

"We haven't got much other choice. There's only this one road."

The donkey stopped again and looked back at the passengers in the wagon. This time it didn't bray or lay its ears back.

"Now what?" The old man climbed over the back of the seat and sat next to the woman. He scrinched his eyes to see ahead of the donkey. The path had narrowed to a point and disappeared into a mass of tree roots. "Road's gone." He pulled another potato from the sack and took a bite out of it.

"It's there, no doubt upon it. The forest just doesn't want us going through is all."

The old man chuckled. "It ain't met you yet." He inspected a dark spot in the spud he was eating, tossed it over the side of the wagon, and pulled another potato from the bag.

"No, they haven't. And I'm not really in the mood for polite introductions. Take the reins." The woman climbed down from the seat and strode purposefully to the place where the road was blocked.

"You'd best be letting us through," she said to nothing in particular but also to everything around her.

The roots expanded slightly, as if taking a deep breath, and wove themselves tighter around each other.

"You have no idea who you're dealing with," said the woman, "and you don't want to be tryin' me, as I am in no mood for shenanigans." She gave them the look her sons had learned meant it was time to be finding something else to do in a location where their mother wasn't.

The roots did nothing.

Folding her arms across her chest, the woman tapped the toes of one foot and set a glare upon the thick wooden tendrils.

They shrunk a little, but still the roots remained where they were.

There have been sayings about a look that could kill, and there have been sayings about looks that freeze, and more sayings about looks that could cause the wind to stop and the earth to reconsider the direction of its rotations. The woman looked at the roots with an amalgamation of those sentiments plus a few of her own. She tapped one finger against a crossed arm. She said nothing, which, as it was understood by her own offspring and now by the trees and their roots, was worse than if she'd said anything.

You could almost hear the air wheezing out through the roots as they shrunk and shriveled and slunk back, revealing the road once again.

The woman went back to her seat, took the reins from the old man, clicked her tongue against her teeth, and signaled the donkey to continue their journey down the path.

They traveled for a good part of the morning, their progress slowed somewhat by the road winding around a great deal more than necessary. However, while the path might have done its best to be a hindrance, there were no more obstacles to block their way. In fact, there were a few times the woman was sure she saw twigs and sticks rolling themselves off to the side of the road and out of their way.

The donkey's ears perked at nearly the same time the woman heard the excitement ahead. A cacophony of curses and barks and mewling and chattering in strange voices and languages.

"Sounds like a ruckus ahead of us," said the woman, "within which we can be fairly certain those boys are somehow involved."

Tired of following the road that would surely take them in the wrong direction, the woman snapped the reins and guided the donkey off the path and directly towards where the noise was coming from. Miraculously, a new path appeared as shrubs and trees scuffled aside.

The woman nodded towards the greenery. "Thank you," she said.

The trees rustled their leaves in reply.

"These trees've been havin' fun with us," said the woman aside to the old man, "but I expect those ahead of us won't be frolicking around. We're going to be seeing what gave this forest its name."

The magpie flitted to the woman's shoulder. "Woot!" it said in agreement, then flew back to the donkey, alighting between its large ears again. The donkey shook its head but was unable to dislodge the bird.

Thirty-Four

"We dares you to try that again!" the aoseelie warned the Willow.

The tree cried, "I'm only trying to help the little thing."

"No you ain't," said the aoseelie. "You was reaching up to grab 'er. Prob'ly plannin' on havin' 'er for stew."

Wunmor sat on a thick, top branch of a tree that wasn't a likho, with fairies around, above and below her. Unseelies and aoseelies, some of them with their long and tangled green hair wrapped around pieces of tree so their oversized hands and feet could be free to kick and punch at anything that ventured towards the Moggybairn.

On the ground below, cats hissed and mewled. Some were directing their consternations towards the league of likhos that surrounded them, while others menaced the hobgoblin that stood in their midst. Some of the felines caterwauled to the world in general just because it was fun and felt good.

Edwina, in the uncomfortable center of the mob of cats, clutched the bag of eyes that hung on her belt, slapping her feet at any that came too close. She'd tried riding the pig out from the swarm, but couldn't hold on when it wriggled and squealed and bounded back to the comforting open arms of Burnt. She looked towards the Moggyfrau and the sleek black cat sitting on a rock. They appeared to be amused and greatly enjoying the events unfolding before them, which irked the goblin.

"Confound you, ya bleakin' little witch! I dares ya ta come a bit nearer and then we'll see what's amusin' and what's not."

"I believe I'm enjoyin' myself right where I am," said the Moggyfrau.

"You's scared?" Edwina narrowed her eyes and wrapped a toothy grin across her goblined face.

"Only that I might lose my appetite if'n I gets too close to that bodily odor you carry about."

The black cat snorted and covered its nose with a claws-extended paw.

"You's just jealous! You's – " Edwina espied a small fluff of white sneaking up behind her. "Get back ya vittled varmint!"

She kicked at the creeping kitten, who swatted back at her with its tiny, yet still very sharp, claws.

Meanwhile, the likhos, ignoring the cats and goblin and witch, continued their efforts to snag the Moggybairn.

"No, I don't have vines," snapped the Chokeberry. "What shrub has vines?"

"Well, we need something to reach up and grab her with," said the Oak.

They'd tried throwing acorns and berries and cones at her, but Wunmor just giggled and slapped them back at the likhos. Her aim was good and after several stings and bites from their own weaponry, the goblin-trees stopped throwing them.

Half-hanging from the branch, Wunmor felt the limb shudder. She pulled herself up and found her brothers sitting on either side of her.

"Hello!" she said.

"You's can talk?" said Dissun.

"Of course I can talk," said Wunmor. "I'm a kitty-cat and all kittie-cats can talk." She swung down below the branch again, making faces at the likhos.

"You's only parts kitty." Dudderun laid on his belly on the branch and leaned down to talk to his sister. "You's human, too."

"I like the kitty part," said Wunmor.

"Well, I can sees why," said Dissun, who laid in the same position as his brother. "But mum says it's time to come on home."

"Where? I don't see her anywhere." Wunmor giggled, pulled herself up and climbed to the branch above her brothers.

"Well, she tolds us, and we're your big brothers, so's you gotsta do as we says." Dissun felt ridiculous saying it.

"No!" squealed Wunmor, and she scurried to an even higher branch.

"Well, it was worth a try," said Dudderun as the two boys pulled themselves upright on the branch.

"Yeah," Dissun nodded, looking around them. "Should'a knew it wouldn't work. Never worked where our uncles tried it on us."

"Nope, it sure didn't," Dudderun was also looking around. "I guess we'll just have to see what she does."

"Aldbrecht said he'd catch her if'n she tried to run aways again."

"Yeah... I'm still a bit nervous about that. He was a might too quick to be agreeable upon it."

"Ah," said Dissun, "he won't eats her. At least not until tomorrow when the full moon's done."

Above them, Wunmor had run to the outer reaches of her branch. It dipped under her weight and the Oak jumped, reaching up and just missing her as she skittered back to the middle of the tree. She did this over and over again, laughing while the likhos grew as angry at themselves as they were at her.

"She's truly one of us," said Dissun, proudly watching his baby sister happily antagonizing the goblin-trees.

"That's for sure somethin' to be proud of seein'," agreed Dudderun.

They watched for a bit, enjoying the entertainment, grinning grins that matched the one on their sister's face. But, after a bit, they looked at each other.

"Well," said Dissun, "I s'pose we'd better be getting' to our plan."

"You's right," said Dudderun. "As much fun as all of this is, we do be wantin' to be goin' home sometime in the near future."

They nodded, gave each other a thumbs-up, and jumped from their branch.

Dudderun aimed for and landed on the Redwood. He dodged and dove away from the stick fingers that grabbed at him, and climbed up the tree's trunk until he was standing on top of its head. Reaching into his pocket, he pulled out a large pinch of cat hair and sprinkled it on the tree. As the Redwood sneezed and tried to brush the hairs from its face, Dudderun jumped off and onto the next closest likho.

To the other side of the league, Dissun was doing the same with the Oak. The boys jumped from one likho to the other, dropping cat hair on the heads of each one. When every likho was sneezing and wiping at its face, the boys jumped to the ground.

"D'ya see the burned one?" asked Dissun. "The one that tried to eats us?"

"No," answered his brother. "But we can get to takin' care of that one later."

They nodded in agreement, found the tree their sister was in, and climbed back up it.

"Come sit with us and watch this," said Dissun, patting his hand on the branch.

Wunmor, having watched her brothers jumping from tree to tree, felt they were more like her than not, and decided to trust them. She plopped her bottom on the branch between them. Also having watched the boys hopping from likho to likho, the unseelies and aoseelies, feeling both impressed and curious, swarmed around the Moggybairn and her brothers.

Edwina was in the midst of a string of curses aimed towards the Moggyfrau when she was interrupted by a howling wail that shivered every timber for across the Goblin Forest, and probably beyond. Abruptly, she stopped and turned towards the sound. She wanted to say something, but it was so horrific, her goblin brain shut down and refused to produce anything but a series of "whahs" and "rrurrerrs" and "mumblemumummfpts". She finally gave up and let her tongue recede to its hiding place in the back of her throat.

"Oh…" said the Moggyfrau. "Something tells me those boys had some leftover hairs." She made a quick hissing sound, and every cat abandoned their menacing of Edwina and ran to take cover behind their witch. Even the sleek black cat ducked behind her. they weren't frightened. They were, after all, cats. And the Moggyfrau's cats, at that. but, even so, they all felt it was best to let the witch be in front of the horde.

"It's all over me!" cried the Willow, thrashing at its face. "Get it off! Get it off!"

"Something doesn't feel right!" bellowed the Redwood. "Not right at all!"

"Everything tickles, and tingles and aaaiiieeeee!" shrieked the Chokeberry.

The other likhos also had things to say, but there were no words that could quite describe how it felt to have cat hair crawling out of their trunks and limbs, their roots sprouting paws with hooked claws, twigs turning to whiskers and pointed ears, and a long tails growing from knots where branches used to be. The league of likhos rolled and bounced unlike any tree had ever done in the history of trees. Berrys popped off the Chokeberry like tiny red missiles, and acorns threw themselves to the ground, burrowing into the soil with their pointed heads.

"Wheee!" Wunmor clapped her hands together with glee. "They're funny!" she said.

When it was all done, and the dust had settled, many mouths hung open in awe of what stood before them. The Redwood stood tall with red fur covering its body from the top of its pointed-eared head to the claws on its roots. The Chokeberry, while shorter and much more stocky, was the same but with berries dangling from the tips of long whiskers. It tried to say something but what came out was more like the mewl of a cat with a mouthful of dead things. The Oak and the Pine found themselves in much the same predicament, with the Pine sporting an extraordinarily long neck covered in green, spikey hair. The Oak tried to look dignified, but, having apparently received more Manx hair than the others, the short and stubby tail thumping the ground behind it made that impossible.

"Oh, this is the worst day of my liiiiiifffffe," moaned the Willow.

"Oh, dry up!" snapped the Redwood. "We're all having a bad day."

They heard a chuckle, and turned to see Burnt sitting on a rock at the edge of the circle with the pig sitting on its lap.

"Hey!" yelled the Chokeberry to the audience in general. "Which ever of you did this, you missed one!"

Thirty-Five

*T*here was a moment, one filled with the air of possibilities of what could be. Fraught with anger, humiliation, argument and blame. Thick with a building, uncontrollable laughter. Ready to pop with every thought within every head of every cat, fairy, goblin and witch.

But... none of that happened.

Because, just as that moment was about to burst, just as the air was about to explode, a wagon pulled by a donkey with a magpie on its head, and driven by a woman with an old man at her side, rolled into the center of the clearing.

Unseelies and aoseelies alike froze in place. Edwina wished she could freeze but her quaking bones were making her skin flap so much, holding still was impossible.

Cats huddled to the side of the witch that was furthest away from the wagon, cringing away even more when the donkey snorted and shook its head. The Moggyfrau turned to face the newcomers directly, but didn't do more than that.

"Uh-oh…." said Dissun and Dudderun simultaneously.

"Mommy!" said Wunmor. Her bottom wriggled as she prepared to jump from the tree to her mother's arms, but her brothers held her in place.

"It might be best to give her a minute," said Dissun.

"For all our sakes," said Dudderun.

Wunmor flicked her tail unhappily, but stayed put on the branch.

The magpie swooped and perched on a branch sticking out of Burnt's trunk. It nipped a bug from the pig's ear, and the pig gave a happy oink towards its feathered friend.

Aldbrecht sat at the base of the tree where Wunmor and her brothers sat, eyeing the passenger in the wagon, a growl germinating from low in his throat.

The woman handed the reins to the old man. She didn't get out of the cart, but stood, raising herself slowly. She made her hands into fists and placed them on her hips. She looked across the clearing, starting at one end and scanning across to the other. As her eyes reached them, every creature looked down or away. Some shuffled their feet. Others argued with their bladders (a few lost the argument). After visually perusing the scene, her eyes settled on her two sons and her daughter.

"What's going on here?" she said. It was a tone that was just below the level of annoyance where there could be no return, giving the boys a tiny bit of room for an attempt to redeem themselves.

"Well, mum, ya see...."

"We was just tryin' to gets little Wunmor..."

"Oh, never mind," said the woman and she stepped down from the wagon. She reached out her arms. "Come here, little one." Wunmor looked from side to side at her brothers, stuck her tongue out at them, and bounded down into her mother's embrace.

Nobody saw Edwina's ears snap to attention, nor the little bit of a grin that twitched at the corner of her mouth. They didn't see the gleam in her eyes, or the prickles of goosebumps that sprouted across her pocked skin. But the goblin couldn't choke back the cackle as it crawled from her throat. And the Moggyfrau was close enough to hear *that*.

The tiny witch turned to the goblin. "No, you *won't* be havin' her..." She plucked a single hair from her dandelion head and twirled it between her fingers.

"Heh-heh-heh…" Edwina laughed. "I knows her name now. That's all I needs." She turned to the woman holding the baby and reached out a bony arm, stretching her sinewy fingers towards them. "Hands her over. That thing's mine and I'll be a'takin' it with me."

"That's what you think!" yelled the Moggyfrau, raising both her arms above her head, the single dandelion-hair held taut between her hands. "She's mine!"

As the goblin and witch engaged in their showdown, the boys in the tree watched with amazement.

"I ain't never seen nobody go against our mum," Dissun whispered to his brother.

"Me neither," said Dudderun.

Below them, unseen by anyone, the wolf slowly and silently crept towards the wagon.

"You're *him*," said Aldbrecht.

"Who?" said the old man. "What're you talkin' about?" He looked at the wolf approaching the wagon and pulled his body back. "Why's it that you can talk?" His voice rattled and he nervously nibbled at his potato.

"You're the old man who bit me," One paw raised, then set, another raised, then set, as the wolf continued creeping towards the wagon, head down, teeth bared, ears pressed back along its neck. A low growl emanated from deep in his throat, and a single drip of saliva hung on a lower fang.

Dudderun looked at his brother. "We was right. It *was* grandpa who dunnit."

"You'd best watch out, grandpa," Dissun called down. "That there wolf says you bit him and turned him into a vulfusgrump."

"Turned into a what?" said the old man, finally seeing a reason to stop his gnawing.

"*You* – !" snarled the wolf, and it leapt towards the wagon.

"Ack!" yelled the old man and, against what most people would call better judgement, he jumped out of the wagon, realizing too late that such a move wasn't the best idea. He turned and started scrambling back into the wagon, bony knees and elbows moving every which way. "Aiee!" he yelped.

"That's payback for biting me," said the wolf, spitting the old-man taste from his mouth.

"KNOCK IT OFF!" roared the woman. "Everyone. Sit down! And be QUIET!"

Everyone sat. The ones who were already sitting scrunched their bottoms deeper into the trees, dirt and rocks. Nobody spoke. A squeaky bit of flatulence escaped from the back end of Edwina that, in the sudden silence, everyone heard. Wunmor giggled.

"That's better," said the woman. "Now, one at a time, explain what's going on." She turned and pointed at the boys who were opening their mouths. "Not you two." She found a rock and sat down.

Fairies and goblins, witch and humans – everyone in the clearing looked at each other for a very brief moment. Then they all began to speak at once.

"All we's wanted was a bit o'that old goat's milk – "

"It was only a few handfuls of cat hair…"

"Frog eyes! I have frog eyes now!"

" – in exchange for doin' some chores."

"It's *my* bag of eyes, I don't's care a scag about traditions!"

"Woot! Woot!"

"He bit me!"

"You was gonna put her back. "

"I think she's just fine as she is."

"Goat milk!"

"Ain't no curse on me nor these here eyes…"

"I want my own eyes back!"

Ignoring the 'one at a time' directions, it continued this way until most everyone ran out of breath, excuses, insults and explanations. Those who hadn't run out continued to mutter, but kept their voices low. By now the woman was hungry and wishing she had been a bit more clear about time limits. She stood, and muttered something most of everyone wouldn't have wanted to hear, except, perhaps, Edwina who was always in the market for a few new curse words.

"Hand me my things," she said to the old man who was sitting in the back of the wagon rubbing the spot on his shin where the wolf had bitten him. He paused his self-pity long enough to give her the bag, the box, and the plank of wood, then went back to inspecting the depth of the teeth marks on his leg.

With Wunmor on her hip, the woman took the items from the old man, and walked to the middle of the arena. A circle cleared around her without her needing to ask for it. She set the box on the ground in front of her feet, slipped her wrist through the drawstring on the bag of chalk, and wielded the shingle in her hand.

"What's in the bag?" came a voice from somewhere in the crowd, small in its worry that maybe it didn't really want to know the answer.

"Chalk." The woman twitched her wrist, giving the bag a quick shake.

The goblins, likhos and hobgoblin, gasped. Even from their distance, Dissun and Dudderun were sure they heard more than a few rattling orifices pucker and shut tight. Burnt covered its frog eyes.

Aldbrecht chuckled, "I can certainly believe that she is your mother," he said to the boys.

"And," Edwina whined, pointing at the box with a shaking, knuckled finger, "what's in that?"

"You'll be finding out soon enough," said the woman, looking down at the box, "unless we can resolve this peaceably."

A tittering waved through the throng, with words describing the fears of every member slowly rising in a swirling verbal mist. Words like *bogart*, and *demons*, and *worst of all*. And there were questions within the chatter. Questions like *is she a witch?* and *how could she have caught one?* and *does ya think we could snatch it from her quick-like?* The woman put one foot on the box. *Naw, ain't nobody gonna get that from her.*

"I'm not a witch," said the woman, her voice as even as a smooth river with a wicked current beneath. "I'm worse."

"Hah! What's worse than a witch?"

"Hey!" shouted the Moggyfrau. "There ain't no need for disparagement."

"I'll bet she's kin to one've them aoseelies!"

"I'm *certainly* not a fairy," said the woman.

"Then what is you?" This came from a few voices, and was followed by many others saying "yeah…" and "tells us what you is…"

"Oh, no…" said Dissun. "They've asked for it now."

Dudderun nodded. "Might be nice, for once, to be a witness rather than the target."

"True, but nonetheless we best be keepin' our ears open and our bodies low whilst it's happenin'."

With nods of agreement, the boys closed their mouths, hunkered down, and clenched their firmly onto the branch where they sat.

Thirty-Six

*T*he woman took a deep breath, held it, and let it out slowly. Then she spoke. Her voice was low, requiring everyone to be quiet and make an effort to hear. It was something she'd learned from her mother, who'd learned it from her mother, and so on for as long as there'd been mothers.

"I…" she said, "am an angry woman. I've evaded the nets of goblins and seared the eyes of a likho." She looked to where Burnt stood, still covering its eyes. "I've more than several brothers who do as they're told by me and," she nodded backwards over her shoulder towards the old man, "I've kept this old sot full of potatoes for the past too many years." The old man opened his mouth, thought better of it, and shut it closed again. "Just today," the woman continued, "I moved trees simply by looking at them." She let a small, impish smile slip across her lips. "And that's not even beginnin' to discuss my daily chores. I've not enough time in my day for foolishness."

She paused for a moment to let the words sink in. When it was clear nobody was going to attempt a rebuttal, she spoke some more.

"I am a mother who's run out of patience with the lot of you. Goblins and witches and fairy folk always after a pair of daft-between-the-ears boys whose combined sensibility wouldn't fill the head of a flea. And now," her voice grew even lower, "some of you've set your sights on my daughter. Trying even to call her their own. I'll be having no more of this."

She looked evenly across the clearing.

"I know the tales of the old wives and the charms of the old crone. I'm not one you want to be messing with." She held up the bag of chalk and the shingle. "I know how to use these." Likho leaves shook and Edwina's skin warped, trying to hide inside itself. The woman tapped her foot on the top of the wooden box. "And I know *when* to use this."

Edwina looked at everyone around her and decided to take matters into her own hands. "That likho put a curse on your boys!" she sneered, pointing at Burnt.

"Did he now?" said the woman.

"You was there," said the hobgoblin. "You heards him sayin' it!"

The twins sat up.

"Issit true?" said Dudderun. "Is there a curse over our heads."

"Aldbrecht here says he can see it," added Dissun.

The woman looked at the blackened likho. "You cursed them, huh?"

"Yeah…" laughed the Chokeberry. "Tell everyone what you said." It looked over, saw the woman's glare, and rustled itself behind the Oak where it resisted giving itself a tongue-bath.

"I was in a rush, and didn't have time to prepare," said Burnt.

"Tells her!" said Edwina.

"It was towards the both of you," said Burnt. He held the pig a little bit tighter, and the pig oinked in support of its wooded friend.

"Hah!" laughed Edwina. "Not me. Ain't no curse on me…" she muttered the last bit, gently grasping the bag of eyes.

"Admit it. That bag's given you nothing but trouble since that day," said the magpie.

"It's fixed now!" snapped Edwina.

"With my help," said the Moggyfrau.

"In exchange for the old goat!" shouted an unseelie.

"After you tricked the boys into changin' their sister into a Moggybairn," oinked the pig.

Everyone stopped. They looked at the pig.

"Did *you* know it could talk?" the Moggyfrau said to Edwina.

"Never tried to conversate with it," Edwina answered, looking at the pink pig who was smiling at her.

The woman, never having taken her eyes off the burned likho, asked again. "What was the curse?"

The likho looked down at its root-feet and mumbled something.

"What was that?" said the woman.

Burnt looked up. "I said '*a curse upon that thing you carry!*'"

"That's quite a curse!" laughed the Chokeberry.

"Quiet, you berry-brained fool!" the Redwood scolded, knocking the Chokeberry with its thick, red cat-tail.

"See?" said the magpie, nodding its beak towards the bag of eyes. "That thing you carry."

"Also," Edwina eyed the woman and then the sons, "the thing *she* carried. Meanin' her baby."

"I didn't know there'd be two of them," said Burnt.

"Which means…." said the magpie, "it was split in half for them, right?"

"It would appear so," said Burnt.

"It's true, isn't it?" said Dissun?

"We's cursed and that's why we gives you so much trouble," said Dudderun.

The boys grinned at each other, believing they'd come upon reasoning that would excuse them from any transgressions past, present and future.

"Are you kidding me?" laughed the woman. "You two aren't one-fifth the trouble your uncles were when they were your age." She looked at her daughter. "But you…," she gently bumped the baby's nose with her forehead, "you've come upon some new tricks, haven't you?"

"By the sound of it," said the magpie, "it's more like each of you boys is half-cursed."

Wunmor giggled.

The woman shifted the weight of her baby higher up on her hip and spoke to the entirety of the assemblage. "From what I've gathered, there's a question of some bartering going on involving items some of you had no business swapping." With her free hand she pointed towards the likhos. "You aren't involved and can go on about your business elsewhere."

"Wait a minute!" said the Redwood indignantly. It started to say something else, but saw the look upon the woman's face. "Oh, never mind," it said. "We'd rather be somewhere else anyway." It turned to leave, whipping its newly acquired tail. Ears twitching and fur ruffling, the rest of the league followed.

"But what about all this cat-hair and tails and stuff?" whined the Willow.

The Redwood, along with the rest of the league, ignored the whining and shuffled off to another part of the Goblin Forest, preferably as far away from the woman and her wrath as they could get.

"Not you." The woman pointed at Burnt.

Burnt stayed, clutching the pig and avoiding any eye contact with the woman.

"You… the fairies in the tree. Get down here." The woman pointed at the ground in front of her. None of them wanting to be the first in line, they made their way to the clearing in a shifting, huddled ball of arms and legs and tangled green hair. "You tall ones," she said when they were standing in front of her, "are you by chance the reason all the boys' chores have been getting finished and done?"

"Yes, ma'am," said the unseelie standing at the front of the group. "But it wasn't nothing nefarious. We done it in exchange for the milk from the old goat." The unseelies all nodded earnestly.

"And what about you?" the woman said to the shorter fairies.

"We's aoseelies, ma'am," said the one standing closest to the woman's feet. "We ain't had nothin' to do with anything. Not least until Wun—" it glanced at Edwina, "the baby here showed up in our den."

"And even then all's we did was makes it so she could talk," added an aoseelie from somewhere within the throng of hundreds. "We ain'tn't done nothin' wrong and, if ya don't mind, we'd like to be's like them likhos and head on back to our home."

"Is that true," the woman asked the unseelies.

"Yes'm," they chorused.

"Get on with you then," she waved at the aoseelies, and they hastily scampered away.

The woman turned to the wolf. "Since you helped the boys, you can stay if you like," she said, "but any further encounters you need doin' with Grandpa will wait until after I'm done. Agreed?" Aldbrecht nodded and sat for the duration of what came next, but he kept one eye on the old man just for the pleasure of causing some unease for the man who had bit him.

Next, the woman addressed the Moggyfrau. "I suppose you're the reason my little one's grown the parts of a cat?"

"I did have somethin' do to with that, yes," said the Moggyfrau. Unlike the others, she stood as tall as her small, round body allowed. She looked up at the woman, meeting her eyes.

"My boys should know better than to be dealin' with a witch," said the woman. "So I've no quarrel with you. But I am hoping we can come to some sort of agreement."

The Moggyfrau nodded and sat back down. But, still, she kept her eyes on the box under the woman's foot.

"You." Now the woman was looking at Edwina.

The goblin's ears shivered, but she stood her ground. "That baby's mine," she sneered. "I knows its name. And that's the law."

"Who's law?" asked the woman, raising an eyebrow.

Edwina's mouth opened, closed, opened and closed again. Her shoulders dropped and she kicked at the dirt with one of her scabby feet. "So much for bein' teammates," she muttered to herself. "Untrustworthy vermin." Then she looked up. Her gnarled hand went to the bag on her belt. "I gets to keep my bag o' eyes, though."

The woman rolled her eyes. "Yes, you can keep your bag." Then she said, clearly so that everyone could hear, "I am going to set things right, and you are going to abide by what I say."

"And what if we don't?" said someone, nobody knew who.

"If you don't, I'll show you what's inside this box."

The donkey trotted at a quicker pace now that it was heading towards the farm where it knew there would be bales of hay.

"Too bad grandpa had to stay behind," said Dissun.

"Well," said Dudderun, "he turned that wolf into a vulfusgrump, so it's only fair that he gots the favor returned and now's a werewolf."

"Good thing it's the last night of the full moon, so we'll be seein' him tomorrow," Dissun thought aloud.

"Gives us time to set up a good welcome back," said Dudderun, and the boys grinned at the many ideas swirling in their ten-year-old brains.

"I'll bake him a potato, and that'll be that," said the mother sternly.

"He's gonna be gone every month for three days?" asked Dissun.

"Looks that way," said their mother.

"I'm sure I wouldn't wanna be in that brick house with that vulfusgrump and him at the same time," said Dudderun.

"We're agreed upon that," said Dissun, and he laughed, "I'm bettin' them hogboons're gonna be movin' right quick when droppin' off them baskets."

The thought of the baskets with food reminded the boys they hadn't eaten since the day before, and their stomachs churned.

Getting his mind off the emptiness of his belly, Dissun said, "Funny how that bag o' eyes turned out to just bein' some sorta keepsake."

"The way that goblin acted," said Dudderun, "you'd've thunk it had some magic about it or somethin'."

"I wouldn't be too sure about that," said the woman. "Keepsakes and magic often go hand-in-hand. It all depends on whose hand the keepsake is in."

Dissun and Dudderun spend the next few minutes thinking of goblin hands, goblin eyeballs, and what kinds of magic could be made when the two came together.

"What was in the box?" said Wunmor.

It had taken a bit for the woman to get used to the idea that her infant daughter could walk and talk. *Although*, she thought, *it's nice that there won't be any more diapers.*

"Nothing," the woman smirked.

"It's empty?" said Wunmor.

"Nothing in there but your imagination, which can sometimes be your best friend, but other times can be the most dangerous weapon of all."

"You sure got 'em to fix everything right quick with that," said Dissun.

"Yeah," said Dudderun, "Wunmor's got reg'lar human legs now."

"I'm glad I got to keep my ears though," said the Moggybairn. (She had been returned to mostly her human-self, but since there was still cat in her, she was still a Moggybairn.) "And the Moggyfrau said I'm welcome to visit her anytime I want."

"We'll be seeing about that," said Wunmor's mother.

"Maa!" said the old goat trotting behind them.

The End

~~ until the next adventure ~~

Keep reading for a preview...

The Goblin's Castle: The Goblin Chronicles Book 2

One

W unmor sat on the water-drenched log and plucked a frog from the pond.

"Froggy!" she squealed, and tossed it back into the pond. She reached for another.

"Is there nothing you can do to make her stop that?" the King Toad croaked, perturbed.

"She don't listen to us," said Dissun. The rock he sat on jutted out into the pond to where, he hoped, more fish would be. A string dangled lazily from the stick he was using as a fishing pole.

"You just gotta wait 'til she gets tired of the game," said Dudderun. He gave his fishing-stick a jiggle, hoping to lure a fish to the piece of cheese stuck on the hook at the end of its string.

"Well, it's disrespectful," the toad muttered, glaring at the small girl.

"Better'n havin' her kissin' 'em like all them other girls do," said Dissun.

Dudderun shook his head. "Won't never understand none of that."

"Oh, I don't know," said the King Toad. "Now and then there's a prince hiding amongst us. It's a fair trade, putting up with the kisses, just to be rid of the freeloaders."

"You ought to be thankful," said Dissun. "If our mum hadn't gone and asked that seelie to fix things all up, you'd still be surrounded by clams floatin' around with frog eyes in 'em."

"That's true," said the King Toad, straightening himself as much as a frog can do. "Still, it's a nuisance." *However*, he thought, *I should stop by the farm and thank that woman someday. There's not too many people who can get a seelie to fix a broken charm. Probably a wise idea to be on her good side.*

Dudderun looked into the basket that sat on the rock between him and his brother. It had a few fish in it, but was still less than half full.

The twin boys actually had much longer names. One of them was Cor'Nan'Deagun'Lug'Maod-Has. The other was Ran'Ousa'Erult'Antach-Lain. Other than their mother, who could tell them apart by the instincts only a mother has, nobody was quite sure which was which. When the taxman heard about their birth and came around to add them to his records, he'd asked the man of the house what name the infant boys went by. He should have asked the mother, but instead relied upon the grandfather for the information because, well, he wasn't a woman and therefore would know. Having only shortly before recognized his boiled egg was actually a potato, the grandfather was happy to oblige. The old man pointed to one of the infants, "dere's dis-un." Then he pointed to the other one. "And dere's d'udder-un." The taxman had thought the names were rather odd, but he wasn't about to confirm such important information by asking their mother who was, obviously, a woman. And so, Dissun and Dudderun were entered into the book as the names of the twins.

"How much is in there?" asked Dissun.

"Not nearly enough," Dudderun answered.

"I sure do miss havin' them Unseelies helpin' out," said Dissun.

Dudderun shook his head and jiggled his stick again. "Me 'n you both."

The King Toad laughed, sounding like a fat cricket had lodged in his throat. "Serves you right."

The unseelies being referred to were a group of twelve skinny fairies, with skinny legs and arms, overly large feet and hands, and toes and fingers that seemed to be in a constant battle as to which could be longer.. They had long, stringy hair and wore tunics that looked like bedsheets. After capturing the boys with the intention of feeding them to the likho (a goblin we'll meet later in this story), and after the boys had escaped, and after they'd learned the boys had a goat that was quite old and produced milk that was as sour and unpalatable as you'd expect once you'd met the creature, they'd decided it was better to enjoin upon an agreement. They, the unseelies, would do the boys' chores in exchange for the milk that came from that particular goat, which they found to be quite delicious and could bring on the most enjoyable inebriation if consumed in the proper (copious) amounts.

"Yeah, well…," Dissun groused, "You'd've thunk they'd've been a bit more loyal to us, what with us introducin' them to that old goat and all."

"They's all fat 'n happy now," said Dudderun, "gettin' all the milk that old goat can give, just for doin' the chores which we used to do fer nothin'."

"Leavin' us free to be fishermen and babysitters."

"I don't know how much you two can call yourselves fishermen," the King Toad said. He pointed at the basket. "You're more like… like…," he struggled to think of a word that would be descriptive of someone unable to catch a fish and that would also be a proper insult, but no word came to mind. He flicked out his long tongue, caught a fly, and munched on it for the next few minutes while he wondered whether it was worth finishing that thought.

"I don't mind the fishin' so bad. It's the babysittin' that's too much," said Dudderun. "It's near impossible, keepin' a keen eye on her."

"Speaking of which," said Dissun, "where is she?"

The boys looked at the vacant water-drenched log.

"Dang it all!" said Dudderun, scanning the banks of the pond. "Wunmor! Where'd you get to?"

Wunmor had also gotten her name when the taxman arrived and again sought such information from the man of the house (the grandfather) rather than the woman (the mother) who actually knew and understood the words she was speaking as she spoke them. Like her brothers, Wunmor had been given a much longer name by her mother, but since the taxman didn't record it only she and her mother knew what it was. Instead, when the grandfather pointed at the infant and said, "dis here's one more," the taxman shook his head at the odd name and wrote 'Wunmor' in his book.

"Wunmor!" shouted Dissun. He looked at the King Toad. "Did you see where she went?"

The King Toad swallowed his overly-chewed fly. "Nope," he said, smacking his thin lips.

Dissun looked at the deepest part of the pond. "You don't suppose she fell in, do ya?"

"Nah," said Dudderun. "She'd be back out quick-like. Remember, she's still part cat nowadays and cats don't like water none."

"I s'pose yer right." Dissun scratched his chin, then set his fishing-stick on the rock and pulled in its string. The cheese on the end was gone. "Which means we's gots to find her b'fore she gets too far."

"Dang it all!" Dudderun said again, wishing he was allowed to use better curse words like the ones his grandpa used.

Without much choice to do otherwise, the twin brothers set their fishing-sticks and the basket aside, and scooted off the rock to look for their baby sister.

Two

"*I* gotcha now!" Edwina cackled, pulling the drawstring around the sack and tying it tight. Standing back, she took measure of the thing: with Wunmor inside it was about almost as big as her own goblin self. She hoisted the bag and tried to swing it over her bony shoulder, but with the kicking and giggling coming from inside, it was a futile effort. She decided to drag it behind her instead.

The thing about Wunmor was that she had recently been a Moggybairn, or a cat-baby – turned into such when her brothers sprinkled her with the hairs from the cats that lived with a witch called the Moggyfrau. She'd spent a good deal of time being a Moggybairn, enjoying the combination of cat and baby human skills and viewpoints. Her mother, we'll say *encouraged*, the witch to return Wunmor to her human baby form, but the little girl had kept some cat essences: the attitude, the ears and the lack of a need for a diaper. This did cause some confusion for humans, because humans expect a human baby to be something that can't walk, can't talk, and needs assistance in everything nearly they do. Animals, however, readily accepted this human baby with all her abilities because, in the animal world, most babies (excepting those who live in a pouch attached to one of their parents — which we're going to do our best not to discuss) are very capable of walking, talking and needing very little help.

Cats grow up faster than humans so, even though it had only been a short while, Wunmor was now a toddler. However, because of the cat-part of her, she was much more agile than most human toddlers, and she could talk much better than them, too. She fit very well into the animal world, and very much enjoyed the confusion she caused in the human world.

The thing about goblins is that they do not like cats. Not in any way, shape or form (unless dead) — or smell, as on this occasion the goblin Edwina was experiencing, due to Wunmor being a Moggybairn and still very much part cat.

"You's're gonna get me a nice and dandy reward," she said between gags, giving the bag a hard jerk. Her eyes watered at the cat-smell coming from the baby in the sack, but she persevered.

Sorcha Monk

Sorry, but that's all for now.

But don't worry… you'll be able to read

The Goblin's Castle: The Goblin Chronicles Book 2

in Fall, 2024

Alphabetical index of characters

Aldbrecht: A wolf who was bitten by a grumpy old man and now turns into a curmudgeon when the moon is full. Because he is polite, he lives away from his wolf-pack during this unfortunate change. (see: vulfusgrump.)

Aoseelie: A fairy. Looks like an unseelie, but a fraction of the size. Lives underground in the woods. Travels in large groups. Unknown whether it can be trusted. (see: fairy)

Bag of cat tails: The bag Edwina gave her daughter when she took back the bag of eyes with her own mother's and grandmother's and great-grandmother's (and so on) eyes. They are not the kind of cat tails you will find growing at the edge of the pond.

<u>Bag of eyes</u>: According to the tradition followed for generations upon generations, when a daughter reaches a certain age, a goblin hag removes her own eyes and puts them in the bag and gives the bag to said daughter. The bag contains the eyes of every previous hag in the family lineage. Edwina carries hers on her belt.

<u>Burnt</u>: A likho who made the error of turning into a tree in a field of manure. Possibly Edwina's friend, but would never admit it. Is more civilized than most other likhos, but since it's a goblin it still can't be trusted. (see: likho)

<u>Dissun</u>: Dudderun's twin brother. Likes to find ways to get out of doing chores. Isn't keen on being a babysitter. Possibly can't be trusted.

<u>Dudderun</u>: Dissun's twin brother. Likes to find ways to get out of doing chores. Isn't keen on being a babysitter. Possibly can't be trusted.

<u>Edwina</u>: A goblin hag. Skinny, knobby legs and arms. Large hands and large, flat feet, with long and gnarled fingers and toes. Saggy skin, that sometimes has to be lifted up if she

needs to run very fast. Large ears with lobes that hang to the ground. Pocked, warted speckled skin. Jagged teeth. Only a few hairs on her head, all of which grow out of a single, large wart. Standing straight, she would almost reach your knees. Can't be trusted.

Fairy: There are lots of kinds of fairies. In this book, you'll find the fairies called seelies, unseelies and aoseelies. There may very well be other fairies flitting around, but they aren't part of this story. However, there's a chance there might be some in future books of the *Chronicles*, you can never be too sure. In general, it's a good idea to never trust a fairy.

Goblin: Creatures of varying sizes, shapes and features. Greedy. Sneaky and self-centered. Fears anything to do with reading or writing. Dislikes cats that are alive, fairies, humans, other goblins... pretty much dislikes everyone and vegetables. Fond of gems, jewels and precious metals. Love tender, juicy babies. Can't be trusted, and they hold this fact as a badge of honor.

Goblin Forest: A forest where so many goblins live, they've claimed it to be theirs. Nobody cares enough to challenge them on it.

Grandpa: Dissun, Dudderun, and Wunmor's grandfather. Tells stories. Likes potatoes. Grumpy. Trustworthiness is questionable, especially when it comes to the stories he'll tell you.

Hag: A female goblin. This is not an insult.

Hobgoblin: In some places, hobgoblins are different than goblins. In Goblin Tales, hobgoblins and goblins are the same thing. Goblins often call themselves a Hobgoblin when they put on a red cap.

King Toad: The king of the toads/frogs who live in the pond near the farm. Unknown whether he can be trusted.

Likho: A goblin that can turn into a tree. Can't be trusted. Also known as a tree-goblin, and since they are goblins, they most likely cannot be trusted.

Magpie: A annoying bird. But also smart. Don't bother trying to trust it, as it will only do whatever it wants to do, regardless of whether you're trusting it or not.

Mildred: Edwina's daughter. Not very careful with her belongings, especially the keepsakes. Can probably be trusted as much as any goblin, which isn't much.

Moggybairn: A baby that's been turned into a half-cat. (see: Wunmor)

Moggyfrau: A tiny witch. She is round, with a head like a dandelion. You can tell she is very powerful because she has lots and lots of cats. Can be trusted to be a witch.

Morris: Edwina's husband. Mostly unimportant whether you can trust him, but it's probably better not to, seeing as how he is a goblin.

Old goat: A goat on the farm who is incredibly old, and its milk is especially delicious to unseelies. As trustworthy as any goat on a farm could be.

Seelie: A fairy. Looks a lot like an unseelie, but more delicate. Likes to go swimming in the pond at midnight. Prefers to be solitary. Distant kin to the unseelie and aoseelie, but to say so is an insult to the unseelie and aoseelie. Can't be trusted. (see: fairy)

Unseelie: A fairy. Skinny with long, tangled green hair. Long legs and arms, with big feet and hands. Wears a tunics that look like an old bedsheet. Stands about as tall as your shins. Lives in the tall grasses. Will do nearly anything for a jug of old goat milk. Travels in small groups. Unknown whether it can be trusted. (see: fairy)

Vulfusgrump: A wolf who's been bitten by an old man. For three days at every full moon, the vulfusgrump turns into a curmudgeonly old man. Unknown whether it can be trusted, but since it's a wolf you probably shouldn't test your luck.

Woman: Dissun, Dudderun's and Wunmor's mother. She is possibly the most powerful person in 'The Goblin Chronicles', but nobody has the slightest inclination to test her and find out for sure. Can be trusted to do what a woman/mother needs to do. (aka: mother, mum, Mommy)

<u>Wunmor</u>: Dissun and Dudderun's baby sister, who was turned into a Moggybairn when her brothers sprinkled cat hairs from the Moggyfrau on her. She was subsequently turned back into a baby, but still has some cat features: ears, hissing, arching of the back, and no need for a diaper – so she is *still* a Moggybairn. Trusts everyone. (see: Moggybairn)

To My Readers

Thank you so much for reading *The Goblin's Eyes: The Goblin Chronicles Book 1*. I hope you enjoyed reading the story as much as I enjoyed writing it.

As an indie-author, I would so, so much appreciate it if you could take a moment to leave a review. That's what keeps us writers alive in these literary ventures.

A bit about this story ...

The first chapter of *The Goblin's Eyes* was a short story, but I liked Edwina so much I decided she needed more. And, boy did she have a story to tell. It was so fun to write. I often found myself excitedly telling people what Edwina was doing, as if she was a real person. Well, to me, she *is* a real person. I'm not sure how she'd feel about that, though. So let's keep that between you and me.

With all of my stories, I like to include a little bit of my own family's jokes. My father liked to play games with words. He was a teacher, and as I'm sure we all remember our teachers doing, he would write sample papers so his students could see what they were supposed to be doing, and those papers had to have student's names, of course. Two of his *students* were Dewey Hafta and Ida Wanna. When I was a teacher, I borrowed those for my own sample papers. Dissun, Dudderun and Wunmor are my nod to Dewey and Ida, and to my father.

About the author

When I read a story, I like knowing a little bit about the person who wrote it. So, here's a little bit about me...

I was a middle school teacher for almost 20 years, but that was in another life. Nowadays, when I'm not writing, I spend my time playing in the clay with pottery, riding my motorcycle, walking my dogs, and bowing down before my cats.

I love the weird things that our imaginations can create, and I'm always open to a tale (long or short) that will make me laugh – and maybe give me some strange dreams. I believe that, while sometimes it's good to have a moral to a story, there are other times that it's good just to have a fun time. No morals. No lessons. Just an enjoyable way to spend your time and imagination. I think (I hope!) that's what you find in my stories.

At the time I am writing this, I live in the town where I grew up. It's in a desert, near a river with a wildlife refuge, and surrounded by mountains. Growing up, there were always dogs and cats in my family. We had a couple of Mustang horses that we rode bareback, and lizards and tortoises and birds… but mostly dogs and cats. I love taking my dogs to the river, where they can run up and down the beach and chase each other over who owns the stick they found.

For as long as I can remember, I have enjoyed reading. I was the kid who always had a book, and my library reading-punchcard was full of holes. Today, I'm the one with the ebook (because I can't carry all the books I want to read). I have always loved stories – especially the good ones – and I hope that for you, *The Goblin's Eyes: The Goblin Chronicles Book 1* has been a good one.

If you have questions, comments, or just want to say *"Hello!"* I would love to hear from you. You can email me at sorchamonk@sorchamonk.com or find me on twitter @sorcha_monk and on Facebook as Sorcha Monk Author.

Other books by Sorcha Monk

Saving Sun and Moon:
The Quest of the Almost-Goddess

The Goblin's Castle:
The Goblin Chronicles Book 2
(coming Fall 2024)

SORCHA MONK

Made in the USA
Columbia, SC
13 February 2024